THE MIRROR IN T

MICHELINE AHARONIAN MARCOM

THE MIRROR IN THE WELL

DALKEY ARCHIVE PRESS   CHAMPAIGN & LONDON

Library of Congress Cataloging-in-Publication Data

Marcom, Micheline Aharonian, 1968–

The mirror in the well / Micheline Aharonian Marcom. — 1st ed.

p. cm.

ISBN 978-1-56478-511-4 (acid-free paper)

1. Triangles (Interpersonal relations)—Fiction

2. Desire—Fiction. I. Title.

PS3563.A63629M57 2008

813'.54—dc22

2008012295

www.dalkeyarchive.com

The lines on page 42 are taken from the poem
"Sit by Me" by Khalil Talaqani, from *Love's Alchemy: Poems
from the Sufi Tradition*, trans. David and Sabrineh Fideler
(Novato: New World Library, 2006) p. 155.

Partially funded by a grant from the Illinois Arts Council, a state
agency, and by the University of Illinois, Urbana-Champaign

Designed and composed by Quemadura, printed
on permanent/durable acid-free, recycled paper,
and bound in the United States of America

What god is in that body I do not know; I do know
that a god is there. **OVID.** *Metamorphoses*

Truly good and indeed divine things are alive and active
outside you and should be let in to work their changes.
Such incursions formally instruct and enrich our lives
in society; no prophet or healer or poet could practice
his art if he did not lose his mind, Sokrates says. Madness
is the instrument of such intelligence. More to the point,
erotic *mania* is a valuable thing in private life. It puts
wings on your soul. **ANNE CARSON.** *Eros the Bittersweet*

The heart must present itself alone before nothingness,
and alone it must beat loud in the darkness. In your
ears, you only hear your own heart. When it appears
completely naked, that's not communication,
it's submission. For we were made for nothing if
not the little silence. **CLARICE LISPECTOR.** *Soulstorm*

Nothing is gained without a guide, even if one stays up
nights/in study.
Let us die before dying, Bahu, only then is the Lord attained.
SULTAN BAHU. *Death Before Dying*

The human being who trudges along day by day in the
functions of bodiliness and unfreedom receives in ecstasy a
revelation of freedom. **MARTIN BUBER.** *Ecstatic Confessions*

Defending love has always been a dangerous,
antisocial activity. **OCTAVIO PAZ.** *The Labyrinth of Solitude*

THE MIRROR IN THE WELL

1

The girl and her lover meet for the first time at a pub downtown. They had arranged this meeting over the telephone the week before and they share a liter of beer and soon the girl is high from the alcohol and she thinks that you are not beautiful and awkward and you speak slowly, as if speech were something to be careful with, like a man handling small glass figurines.

The motel is pink and a cheap one on L Street run by Pakistanis and you pay in cash and she will realize after you fuck her for the fourth time (but not today) that you always pay in cash and you hold her against your naked form in front of a mottled grey mirror and you say how beautiful she is and the girl moves her gaze to the reflection, to the image of a woman with long dark hair and brown eyes painted black that night, a red bra and black cotton underpants and she is beautiful in the mirror and not recognizing herself: some thing out of a circle of ideas, a blurred picture of eros, and you behind her with your white skin blue eyes and fatty belly pushing into her ass.

(Then later—, months after the girl's husband has discovered the liaison and a year and a half after this initial meeting and she is sitting on the sofa in the living room of her home and looking out at the pine and cypress and beech and alone because the husband has moved out of their home, she will recall this image of herself in the mirror, of you behind her, of her sorrow like an amulet but not only for the ended marriage, something else which she can't fathom or unfathomably put consonant and vowels to (yet?), some silence unletterable alongside her sorrow, some things and notthings which she tries to grasp with the edges of breaths (to make, or to find—like a man makes a tunnel for his underground passage).)

You remove her black shirt her trousers. You fumble with her bra as you had briefly with the snap on her jeans. And she tells you how she doesn't want to fuck you and she doesn't tell you that she has decided she will fuck you the next time but not tonight, hoping in part (there is always shame for the girl) that this means there is more later, around some kind of time-corner, and trained, like a good penitent, to think that the pleasures must be delimited and she says to you that she doesn't want to fuck tonight and alright, you say, spread your legs and let me eat your cunt.

You open up her cunt with both of your hands, pull the outer brown-pink labia the smaller and wrinkled black-pink inner labia apart and she is uninitiated, the thirty-nine-year-old girl who has been fucking since eighteen and the mother of two boys, but has never had her cunt sucked properly so that her sex becomes an altar and the man prostrate there as she had imagined him many months before this affair (or the other affairs; or in her office when she was lonely and desirous, before she knew her lover, the other lovers) as he is wont to and seeking all of the women to get back inside of their fleshy slits. She is anxious and opens her legs, but not widely, as if you are a medical doctor and putting your face near to her and your instrument inside of her for medical purposes and she has always (a remembered always, because the very young girl-child was unashamed, her cunt opened to the boys and girls during play) hidden the cunt its smells and secretions; crosses her legs and tightens her thigh and buttock muscles. It takes a long time before the cunt begins to secrete its fluids and she wonders who you are: a pervert; a man who fucks whores; a violent man; a liar; perhaps you will use her body, you will arouse her only to put your cock inside and then you will lie to her again and then you will depart and she will be alone and she will be transformed and she will be in pain and ashamed of her desires, her stink.

You are patient and experienced—the hundreds of women and whores before your meeting with this girl in the pink motel late at night, it is eleven o'clock now and you eat suck lick her and she is thinking that she will never come, that what is she doing, what would her husband do if he knew of this transgression and although the husband never sucks her cunt and she has never orgasmed into a man's mouth before and that who are you, you are dangerous; that she is in a motel with a stranger, that if her husband could see her now while he is at home with their sleeping children that with her legs splayed on the motel bed, wider now than moments ago, and three miles from her home, fucking this stranger, he is eating her pussy better and longer than any man in her lifetime as if he knows how to arouse her and how does he?, as if he knows that she has waited for him and suddenly she knows, thinks it, that she is aroused beyond the point of return, like a girl who has moved off an old and weathered path and that she will come, that he is licking patiently, sucking, pulling on the lips and rubbing the clitoris, that he understands her body's cues, breathstops -starts and she stops breathing and begins again stops and he follows her breathing, he tells her later, and she is silent for the thirty-five minutes while he patiently learns her idiom, sticks his fingers into her vagina and she moves out in and then she wasn't thinking and then she is listening again and he is saying please hold me while he takes his cock into his hands and rubs it with both of his hands and that her leg on top of his leg, his eyes closed and he is grunting rubbing his penis then ejaculating and she asks if he is satisfied, happy that she did not have to suck his cock at his request. He is happy to hold her, he says.

4

She puts her clothes on and sits on the edge of the motel bed, she is feeling guilty now, perhaps by the ease of her adultery, the pleasure of it, she doesn't look into your eyes (has she looked at you at all tonight? or has she simply moved along the path of your vibrations, her scent yours) and tells you that she must go, home to her children and husband who does not eat or suck her cunt and who fucks her infrequently and she masturbates daily and reads the porno books purchased from a sex shop on J Street. Later she thinks how she wouldn't have been so hungry all of these years and eaten more than her share at every meal (the large appetites) if she had been properly and frequently fucked: every day, but this thought comes six weeks later when you fuck her for six hours on a white platform bed in a city hotel where the light comes in through the half-opened blinds in the afternoon and she is sick with a head-cold and tired and can see the highrises in the distance of downtown and will orgasm nine times and sprays you with her vaginal secretions. But now, in this first scene at the motel, you unbutton her just-buttoned shirt and undo her bra again and surprise her that you would like to notfuck her arouse her again with your mouth and tongue; you don't speak while you do it. Your penis is stiff and you don't touch yourself or ask her to suck you as she is still expecting you to, or try to cajole her into allowing you to fuck her, but bury your face in her cunt again and late into the night and she lies there self-consciously thinking that who is this foreign blue-eyed man and that she can't come again—the limits the edges she is accustomed to—and soon

5

she has a second orgasm into your mouth, outsideness inside of the dingy and poorly lighted room—but not as out as she will become with this man who will become her lover, who teaches her the unteaching of the limits, that love is expansive that yearning and its disruptions are as old as the days; that he can bring her to the inside of outness and that she can arrive outward with him on each of the days that they fuck.

At breakfast the next morning. It is the day before her fourteen year wedding anniversary. You and the girl sit together at a local café and you eat your food with your open mouth and your hands the knuckles and fingers are fat and swollen looking, as if you have labored. You are still speaking slowly, stones turn leisurely between each of your words. You tell her that you could love her and she sees the egg whites and yellows in your open chewing mouth. She is repulsed and attracted at the same time, to the moments of the night before, this strange man, slow-speaking and widely eyed and opaque to her with the openness of days and spaces between each word and phrase.

6

You will teach her about whips and small pains in bed. Each time you put your mouth to her cunt she is happy, as if this is what she was born to know and experience and is so lucky, now, in the modern world, to find the man who still worships properly, sucks her cunt with enthusiasm so that the circuit is completed, his mouth her mouth her cunt her open mouth and his and both he and she are filled with the gods.

2

She drives south to see you for your second meeting. She gets lost as she approaches your city and she doesn't think of fucking you because she always thinks of fucking and so is not conscious, in this moment, of her perpetual adult desire, its mark upon her body, and invisible and unremovable. You have Japanese food for lunch, and she looks out the window of the restaurant and tells you of her loss of faith in speech, by how little it communicates, by the lies and half-spokens and the masks of her American brethren and the speech so degraded now, was it ever different?, banal, and she is bored by the middle class, its diversions, by her own lying phrases and postures. Did the gods ever live inside the letters sounds? You seem to understand. Look at her with a look of comprehension. She is struck by this knowing look and knows, feels, that you fall in love with her during this conversation: that she seduces you with her flight of words. Later, on the floor of your workroom, she pulls off from her body as she orgasms and returns, astonished and naked now, understands what she has not understood in her marriage, her husband

7

as blind as she to the forces moving through them and she unable to find its electric breach until now. You have done this to her; you? You give her a second orgasm right before she must leave: you lie naked on the workroom floor with her for hours and the world passes by you and then you are touching her clitoris with your fingers, the speech evaporates and putting your fingers inside of her cunt and she is crying after orgasm, she sobs, and you are not sure what causes the girl this grief and it is not grief, she does not say, for having found you, some profound mystery she has intuited for all of her life and you have taken her across the threshold and she is free. Or simply that you fucked her twice and not the once she had been lucky to get once every two weeks or month up until this today—the one if she'd been a good and obedient girl and wife and office-worker and citizen.

You will be her guide: willing and desirous of fucking as much as she—will eat her pussy five times in a day and she will flow into your mouth, her damp underwear and your body odor on her skin remind her of you for hours. She doesn't shower the next day to remember your fucking scent in her pussy (sticks her fingers inside) and on her neck and the blue-red marks you leave on her neck also, like fat and bruised souvenirs. When she pulls her pants down to piss the next morning, she smells her cunt filled with your day-old semen and she is happier, serves her family breakfast, dresses the children and makes lunches and drives to their school across town and the next day begins inside of its routines.

She returns to that moment in your workroom in the following months in her memory, just as she returns to the image of the girl in the grey and mottled mirror. The woman that she is then, the long dark hair and unshaved pussy naked on the tiled floor on the top of woolen blankets and your labors all around her, wooden boxes and bedside tables and wood shavings on the floor, the beautiful scent of woods as if the ancient trees themselves were present and their years in this dust and you before her: white skin and a white paunch belly; the blue eyes which see differently, one from the other, and so the world is a flat place for your eyes—and your hands which cut and shape and bevel the wood? deep inside her cunt they pull and push her up and back to a lifting-off place. And the language of it is lost to it. She begins to read the old books, the possessions by the gods, *The Thousand Nights and One Night* is by her bedside, to understand, or the devils, how it is that you remade her in your workroom that afternoon in August, carved and cut an ancient woman, your mother, sister and the nymphs on the lintels of old European buildings—the language can hardly say it any longer: but with your cock inside her cunt and you are pushing it in and her orgasm opened a river inside of her and she would like it beyond language you are grunting into her ear, filling her mouth with your tongue, cunt with cock, spittle and urine and a piston inside of its fleshy destiny and she would like to die with you in this moment and to kill you, squeeze the breath from you you ask her to put her hands around your neck as she rides on your cock and you ask without asking,

9

place her hands around your neck and press her white blue-veined fingers into your trachea, cut off the breath then your orgasm and your breathing again and you have not died and she rides you longer until she slaps your face comes on your cock, pisses and cries into your shoulder. And when she is feeling sad and melancholic as she often does at her job and on the week-ends with her family, she remembers that eternal moment, returns to you then endlessly in her dreams and then also in her car as she makes the drive south to your workplace and the floor upon which you will fuck her week after week month after month during your affair.

It is strange to her that no one sees the change in her. What the afternoons in your workroom do to the soul to the skin and eyes and dark hair. She doesn't love you, she thinks, but you have made her into your acolyte. She no longer fears dying, she fears, instead, not being able to lie on the dark tiles of your workroom floor, your mouth pressed to her cunt, her mouth open and the universe inside and outside her mouth the room.

But perhaps as you make her you do make her fall in. The girl *falls in* to love, as if love were, what exactly?, the underground stone palace where the lover has hidden the beloved? the deepest well where the serpent lives? And you expect it, demand it: Stop fucking your husband, you tell her, I can't bear it (fall in to love with me). She stares at you; she is silent and dark looking in the eyes. I love you, you say, and thrust this inside her like your cock: love me back love me back love me only in this possession. Or else? she thinks, she says nothing while he shoves his cock into her again; she is happy free and at ease with him inside her cunt. Or else no black tiles or opened mouth breath; no drive south on the long highway across the brown grass fields in summer, the green shoots in early spring, the bay water bright when she arrives home or grey cloudy and fogged on summer and winter afternoons.

11

3

Once a week the girl makes the drive to your city and her boss thinks that she is in one place and her husband thinks that she is in another, and the children in school, and the two of them: husband boss who don't love her enough or fuck her, are either deceived or disinterested, and she drives the hour south to see you. You don't kiss her when you open the door to your workroom. Your breath smells badly, of garlic coffee and decay. As soon as your mouth is glued to her cunt (thirty minutes later, after the requisite exchange of sentences of hellos and how are yous) she knows that all is right with the world, that you are right, that pleasure is the reason to live; that she loves you desperately; that you love her infinitely; that you are her satyr and she your muse; that you will be together always (which could be an afternoon); eternity. Then you are dressing, saying good-bye, on the drive back toward the bay and her city, she both worries about your scent upon her skin and hopes that it will abide. Then she stops fucking her husband as you demanded it. They don't fuck again in their conjugal bed. What you ask of her she does, how can she do any different? When you are making her, when you are a god and she also is a god, the nymph visiting from the other world is pushing out of her mouth and breast. The nymph's fluids are her own; the nymph's red and pink lips kiss your mouth sweetly. The girl with the dark hair and eyes and you with your blue blind irises. A snake at the base of the spine unfolds in the dark afternoon in the wood dust and motes.

4

You take a trip with her to the north. For her it is business, and for you your wife stopped asking questions many years ago (your marriage is one of habit and bitter convenience and notasked questions) so it matters little whether it is for business or pleasure that you travel. Then you are driving in the car for many hours to return home. On the drive southward from a cold North American city, a snowstorm arrives unforeseen in the early evening. All of the cars and trucks on the freeway come to a halt, as if the highway has been dammed like a river. You are stopped here for eight hours in the night and snow. After the first hour of thinking that at any moment the cars will begin to move, she shuts the engine off. You think that you are adequately prepared because you have lunch leftovers in the car and a bottle of water; you don't worry yet about the duration of the storm. At hour four, she pulls her pants to her knees and you lean over the gear console and stick your face between her legs, licking sucking and straining. It snows and you are cold in the car with all of your winter gear on; she is fully clothed except for her now pulled-down pants. When she comes she is hot for a while; sucks you off then for the first time and swallows your semen. Then she sits on your lap and you put your cock inside of her; she doesn't come like this but she likes to feel you fucking her, it comforts her and then you come for a second time amidst the hundreds of cars stalled and lined up in rows in the black snow on the highway at midnight in the mountains.

Is it that she is becoming addicted to you? to your mouth on her nether mouth, your fingers inside of her, how you read her body, reason it out, follow her breath and notbreath to pull your fingers up, lick the clit, suck it, suck the labia, pick up speed pick up sticks. She is never sure where this will lead, but wants only always to be on her back on the floor of your workroom with her legs spread wide (she has no trouble spreading her legs for you any longer) and the wood dust in her hair and she lives when you have your mouth on her; don't speak to me; fuck me later; put your mouth on me again and again: I am returning, I am healing a wound, it is all so stupid and unsayable in this English: what your tongue does to my clit and soul:—how it falls in: she doesn't say to you.

She puts her fingers inside of her vagina whenever she can and she is alone. She smells herself on her fingers, wipes her scent onto her upper lip, and on the days that she has seen you, or just afterwards, smells you her and your semen in her cunt as it changes and blooms like a flower when she squats to take a piss.

5

Today it is twelve months after your first meeting at the pub
and you are in your workroom and you are showing her how
to make a box with cherry wood and then in the late afternoon you take your clothes off and climb into bed (you purchased a bed for the workroom three months ago). Let me
eat your cunt, you say, after you have asked her if you have
ever sixty-nined together (you cannot recall) and you decide
to do it another day because you don't have much time (you
have to pick your daughters up from school) and so you are
eating her cunt and she is thinking that she can't come and
thinking she ought to focus on her breath and focusing on it
and you are licking and sucking the lips, put your fingers inside her and later tell her how wet she was even though for
the first time in your affair she is unable to come and you
eventually lift your head and pull her by the legs toward you
(the clock, the time on it) and put her legs on your shoulders
and then stick it in her, I can't wait to stick it in you you always say to her on the telephone and fuck her and it feels
good and you come within minutes and she is sobbing and

can't speak and you would like to know what it is and if she is disappointed and she not-speaking has buried her head in pillows and blanket and crying hysterically, a long and relentless grief and an hour later when she is careening down the freeway and hurrying to pick her children up from school and it rains heavily and she imagines herself closing her eyes for only a moment, enough closed eyedness to allow her car to turn into the other cars, a crash, with her eyes closed and obliterated in the rain the metal automobile and I am so tired, she thinks, with nothing but banal violent dramas in my head and my husband left me ten days ago, my lover, today, unable despite his efforts to bring me to the orgasms and the ecstasy I yearn for have yearned for all of my life (since I was the girl masturbating in the bedroom on the sofa behind the closed closet door) and tired also of this theatre in the mind, these ideas which limit and suffer me, like children suffer bullies.

6

That night she dreamed of a planet between planets, red and large and hidden between Jupiter and Uranus. She was afraid in the dream of this lurking and unknown place places like the invisible lines between waters. She had fallen asleep at seven PM and then the dream of the red lurking planet in the black galaxy of nightdreams. Her children traveled with her and she was not seeking her lover in the dream; in this image she was deposited on the red lands the red skies above her and all of it translucent and ochre without trees or red blooms. Not blooded red, but a silvery white red-glow, as if the sun itself had become this orb or the planet was a star emitting light.

18

Then she dreamed that her cunt hair was thinning, like the hair on an old man's head. Then her mother called her on the telephone, she is thousands of miles away in another American country, and she tells her how today she is wearing the Waltham pocket watch which belonged to the grandmother —one of a few items which the grandmother had saved during the war and taken with her out of the old country and into the new—and the fantastic enters into this story—and how her mother feels the spirit of the woman who owned the watch so many years ago and what is the feeling, Maman, she asks her in accented French: of a protection, her mother replies, like an old watch-guard.

He puts his fingers inside her cunt and twoly finds the sensitive place inside of her or she thought while he did it, rams his fingers in out, and some difficult to ascertain sensation, like a coin-size balloon filling inside her vagina and without touching her clitoris she feels as though she will come and that it is strange to come like this and she hasn't before now and the psychoanalyst wrote his theories about hysteria and the hierarchies of female orgasm and then when she thinks she will get off he pulls his hands out and puts his mouth to her and sucks licks pulls on the clitoris until, in moments, she comes into his mouth he pulls her legs up onto his shoulders and shoves his penis inside of her. Time is illusory, a construction like a wall or canonical texts—this book lasts forever her orgasm is like this book this phrase this moment when these words cannot do anything, all of the vibrations are in the blood then, everything she knows is in her fluids and his.

And there are some days when she thinks that she can't breathe without him, that his scent and his body fat and white wide arm around her frame are life itself and that she would gladly sacrifice all of her possessions to feel his breath his cunty breath in her mouth after sex or she thinks without my home my car my grey and white-trimmed house? No, not for it; not for this undelimited breath not for the cunty breath but wants him now has put her children to bed the house is quiet and there is the blare of the television if she wants it and the blare of an erotic novel or her vibrator and porn: but not him himself, his infrequent laughs his long sad unfocused gaze, his joy for the art of woods, his desire for her like he has desired the lakes and rivers of his childhood: not a divorce, but afternoons waning into evening, the interstitial hours of lovers when the drawn blinds and the moving traffic outside only serve to put the world of the lovers, the eternity of the man and woman his face her sex and their breath into relief.

7

She has traveled to another country without him. And in this country the sun shines strongly today and she walks on the streets of the place seeking him and her skin is burnt by the middle of the afternoon and although he is not here she thinks that she will find him here in another language, behind another cuisine culture artifact of ideas and she looks more and more the gringa, the red shoulders nose and forearms, silly girl, she has forgotten her hat and sun cream and she cannot find him, perhaps he is in the taxis which roar throughout the town or he could be behind the foreign visage the language, inside the seed of culture like history or a book which waits, silently, for her to read it tonight.

She is lonely here without him. She is staying in a hotel on the main street of the town and here the buildings are white and the roofs a red tile black in the evenings. She is afraid to go outside alone to eat alone to walk the streets with the foreign language in her ears and she is not sure why she traveled here: for business, or for pleasure perhaps? A vacation so that she could think, she thinks. Or simply she awoke in a foreign country today and the girls are beautiful here, the men stare loudly, and she turns the television on in her hotel room for the noise and company and the television brings the culture from her own country into this one, and a singer sings to her in English and talks to her about what it is she ought to be doing and she thinks that she will turn the light off, watches the television for hours and does not eat because of her fear, which, shy girl, and wonders where her lover is now, if he is in a foreign country, inside of Armenia or Cambodia, and he is hearing a foreign language and using his English to order a beer now and eat a snack of rice chips of lamb breads and is he thinking of her while he caresses the girl's thigh the girl's neck her back and the spaces beneath her brow; and does he now while he sticks his cock into the young and beautiful Armenian and Cambodian girl think of her in this foreign country, his seed is like an inheritance or a letter he sends to her across the lonely spaces which filled now with his semen and her fingers are finding her cunt walls and pushing inside of her body and soon, late at night in this Central American walled white hotel, the girl is coming, she comes now and for him it is one o'clock in the afternoon and the whore waits for him in three more hours at the bar, holds him between her thighs, and they suspend time and she is inside his cock and he does think of her, of his beloved, who left him last week and they both traveling to foreign places and look, she says, I love you across space across time also. Sleeps then, has turned the infernal and loud talking machinery off and waits for the return to her country. Waits to find him again, to see if it is so, that she hasn't imagined him out of the ether, that her lover exists in fact, makes her into another girl and then another, loves her, yes, as if it were possible she thinks: *he could only be something out of my imagination.* Waits to go home and realizes, just as the sleep descends and she ascends into dream: that she came here to remember that she wants to be at home with her children and with her lover also between her thighs on the occasions that time allows it.

8

She is home now in her country and it is strange because in her country she begins to feel the foreigner, as if she becomes a foreign girl, and raised and educated here with English vowels hurrying out between her teeth and yet they seem now strange, fat, lonely and unhappy awkward invitees: here no one invites you inside his home, the guest is unsacred, bread is not broken, *where is the money?* they ask her, *where are your expensive things?* And who are these inhabitants, masked and tight and living behind the faces behind the limits behind the *I am fines Yous?* She cannot be certain, she cannot does not recognize them, or feel their ancient heat.

She takes an airplane to an American city where the people spend their days inside darkened buildings with loud electronic noises and the clacking of chips of bells of eyes moving outside of seeing into eyes to see only the money they could make from the whirring machines. To be rich! they say (and then happy?). Her lover has not telephoned her from his foreign vacation. She attends a business meeting and then returns home and embraces her children and they sleep curled tightly in her bed, they suck at her breasts again because they remember how they used to do it as small children, as babes, when the breast and her gaze were their days' axis.

—I'll divorce him, she says, although she doesn't mean that she will divorce her husband. She has driven the hour to see you and she is angry at you: why are you still married to someone else, why don't you love me, why am I alone in this foreign country? The questions without words are struck across his face; she doesn't hold his hand as she has always done in the shop they visit. She wants to hurt you, she would like to make you suffer, she asks you again and again today and on many days how it is that you could have married such a terrible woman, the overseer, she says, a woman who is cruel and selfish and beats their girls with her unkind words, beats him down also, and he is patient with her, looks directly into her eyes and she looks away; she is harried; she is a harridan; she hates him today; herself also alone in her home masturbating the long evening while he is in another city another country, travels with his family abroad.

He doesn't return, or in her mind he doesn't return, although he has, in fact, returned to his home in his city, has returned to his job, his familial and work duties; calls her when he can; schedules a rendezvous with her for later in the week. But if you are not here today, she thinks, then you do not exist and you are something that I have made up, a girlhood residual fantasy, of the too many romance novels she read as a girl and so she gets herself into her car (manages to rise from the sofa) and drives the distance to the sex shop on J Street. It is a shop run by women and so there are many women inside of it, here she is not ashamed or although a little shy not horribly embarrassed as she was when she first went into a sex store as a college student and rents a porn film and takes it home and doesn't do her office work, puts it onto the television and watches the girls and boys on the film—their masks —and with masks and the moans of artifice, makes herself come six times with a dildo vibrator. What she likes about the fucking girls on the screen is this: that although disingenuous (without love) and not aroused (the desiccate and hairless pudenda), they are not ashamed of their cunts, open the legs wide the labia wide and the cunt is opened and the men shove their lonely lying cocks inside,—and there is something beautiful and true in that publicly performed act: the openness of the form, the integrated body, albeit with ugly adornment (the silicone filled breasts, the too much makeup faces), but nevertheless, a certain kind of freeness which she envies admires even as she comes.

9

She dreamed about you in the early morning hours. The family was not at her home (the children with their father last night) and she went out with friends from work and drank with them; they ate expensive foods; they spoke hundreds of lying and half-lying phrases; and she talked laughed gossiped (the mask) with her friends, stared silently ahead wounded and mute (laughing gossiping the while) with the inside eye and wondering if her work-friends had closed their inside eye and if the mask, like science, is a thing of progress. And in the dream you are at your home with the beloved and she invites her mother and her mother's companion and other people arrive to your home: a film director and actresses from magazines and her childhood friends and you are in your room reading during the party and then she is worried that your wife will arrive home soon and knows how particular your wife is about your house and so she begins cleaning up the house for you, and there is black hair covering the sink, as if someone has cut her hair over the basin and she is wiping up the black corpses—your daughter's?—for the

27

eternity of a dream moment and then your wife arrives home and she is a blonde (dyed) and her eyes are blue which is not how your wife looks and you are talking together and you are trying to please her and she realizes with the kind of grief that dreams can evoke that you will never leave your wife and that even if you did she might then become your hated wife soon enough and you fucking the girls on the side, promising to call them on the telephone for five minutes at this time of day and to love them always and are you a liar? Is the dream a premonition? Or is it only that she has awoken today with a hangover and dark thick bags beneath her eyes and you left a message saying hello darling and I'm very busy let's talk tomorrow and she would like to kill herself, which is, of course, that she would like to wound you with words (but you are not available to talk with on the telephone) and then she thinks that she will think that this has all been for naught, that it has been wrong, that the gods have misguided misaligned her, that now she will be forever unhappy (a Christian with his penance) that you are not a soulmate or truelove or the man she waited for from within her marriage, and even though she is aware the movies and cheap books and magazine portrayals have rendered love like a small thing to purchase for cheap at stores for joy or disease, she can't help but think of Leda's daughter and of the Vizier's storytelling daughter and of how the one city is destroyed in the old story and in the other, the kingdom flourishes. And she would like to cry, but she is unable to; and she would like to disappear but she won't; and she would like to stop feeling this despair and so thinks that she will go to the movies see friends shop eat barter fuck the neighbor's husband: she is like a sow in her mud (of loneliness) and covers herself in it and what of it—it is the disease of her country, and the late night television shows the magazines and movies in cheap collusion with it.

10

The girl in this story is not a girl, for she is now forty years old, and a mother of two children and becoming a divor-cée and she works in a business, wears suits and tight shirts which she pays extra money to clean at the specialty dry-cleaning stores; she pays bills and mortgages and takes her children to their lessons for improvement and cooks them dinners and organizes closets and drawers, discards rubbish and used-up items. The girl looks up from where she is seated on the sofa of her home, and sees what appear to be hundreds of small grey birds who settle into the bushes and then dash out for no reason she can ascertain, settle and dash, rush out and make a V in flight and return, the nexus disas-sembles and the flock explodes into the bush amidst wild cries and flight again and crash again into the brush and singing loudly. And this is not a usual home for the flock; she sees birds daily—the robins and blue jays and loud crows, the fast-green hummingbirds and the great blue heron which flies each morning over her home toward the state park and each evening back toward his home by the sea. But

30

not these. And she then imagines that she sees the flock to-day because today she is feeling forlorn and abandoned, like a small girl, and doubting and the birds are on a long journey, the journey perhaps of their southern flight for the winter and she also would like to travel, would like some kind of flight, would like an outside of her ideas, the labyrinth of codes and conduct which keeps her close, inside of a closed circuit, and it is only her lover, this carpenter in a Californian city, who has undone the tight bands, who has leaked her soul out onto air again, like the small pockets of air beneath the bird-grey wings and lifting them, today, outside of the girl's window and into the sky.

11

She has driven across the empty fields and drying grasses to see you; the warm-gold light on the dried earth, the reds behind her in the reflection on the rearview mirror, the speeding hulls of cars. She is afraid now that her children and husband are not at home (the husband calls her on the telephone to schedule appointments the children's doctor's school and hair; he is living in a rented house in the adjacent town) and your wife and children have left for the weekend and so they will have this time together today, you tell her, come and visit me, and the girl runs out of her home, turns off the lights and water taps excused and begins the drive, a drive which is like a calling, to lie in your arms to feel again this ineffable unmoment, to listen to this sea like a flock of birds startled out of the bush, and after the dinner at the restaurant with you, and after the banal details of daily living have been exchanged, then they are naked again and his mouth is again against her sex and she is happy and all of her doubt and despair fall out through the pores of her skin like the birds rushed from the copse adjacent to her garden at dusk yesterday. Which family of bird were they? Her son will say that they are not robins, for the robin has an orange-red chest and yellowed bill and she wonders where he learnt of robins and why it is that she cannot name this type of bird, she has searched her consciousness for it as she does for the word which she cannot say to anyone as to why it is that she has flown outside of her marriage and taken the sacrifice of marriage and family and the neighbors' sour and pitiable looks when she tells them that her husband has left her and leaving the man who loves her, who has cared for her and the father of her children and to whom she made a vow, betrays him first in the motel on L Street and then weekly for twelve months until he one day out of the blue, like a flock of small grey birds surprising her and rushing out from the copse, asks her if she is having an affair and she does not admit to him that she loves this other and strange working man in another southern city, the man who puts his mouth to her cunt, the man for whom the birds rush out inside of her, and not for him either has she done it—she suffers like a small child when she is alone now in her home—but to return again and again to the unmomented moment when the yellow-billed not-robins, time and outness which is inness, rush out, as if the world and all of her life were limitless and love a tangible flight outside of words and outside of her life as she knew it before: the appointments the rules the limits and doors which opened, like her cunt, only partially and shyly, like adolescent girls with their tight and scared sexual mouths: she needed to live, and she hadn't known until the man with his mouth on her sexual mouth, that she hadn't, that she wasn't, that fucking is aliveness for her, like flight is for the grey birds—she tells the husband a yes, that she has fucked another man.

Put your mouth on me, she doesn't say to the lover but he knows it, puts his mouth on her and she is bleeding today, she tells him, I have my period, and he doesn't speak to her, will not speak while they are fucking, opens her legs and puts his tongue on to her clitoris, he licks her like a small dog, puts his fingers inside of her, pulls sucks and blows on her labia; he is drinking my blood, she thinks, and she is ashamed and afraid, would like to speak to him but he will not speak and so she lies with her legs opened and she is unable to take flight today, she lies on the bed for eternity while her lover pleasures her as he can: with tongue and fingers and eventually cock, sucks and pulls on the labia, licks and wraps the clitoris with his tongue and she has thought that today she will tell him that she must end this affair, that she doesn't love him, that he is difficult, demanding, and at the same time that he doesn't love her enough, does not leave his wife for her, does not provide for her like a mate and she will tell him, she will take her revenge, she has diatribes and colloquial speech and thought patterns to offer him and he offers, as always, incense, his breath on her bleeding cunt, sucks licks and she won't come and then she is off and the legs pulled taught because of this electric current he rides through her body, pulls out and down the gods again and he is her god and she is the nymph at dusk and she loves him and sticks his cock inside of her and while he thrusts she is the man and he has become the woman and the man thrusts and she is fucking him and he is her cunt and the world is his thrusting and her open and tightly enclosed legs and she forgets that she was reasonably lining her life up like magazine articles in a row, or moral Sunday school codes, because he is her center she is alive and breath and everything is good and right and the cosmos wide and joy moves outward stopping only on the end-side of the breath of this phrase of these letters of this girl and her lover on the old worn mattress on the floor of his workroom in a California city.

12

She drives south to see him. She is in her car and driving as she has driven so many times in this book, behind each phrase and each fuck there is first the drive, the speed inside of the machine, the reaching and urge toward her lover, the petroleum purchased, the gasses burned and black airs made blacker and the world perhaps is unmaking itself, the machines, pollutants and plastics, and still the girl will drive to see her lover, which is to say, to fuck him—to see to fuck and to know: myself? she thinks. For joy. And he is pulling her cunt lips open and he knows when (how? from her breath; she tightens her thighs) to push one finger and more fingers inside of her: he licks her patiently, rhythmically, and if she thinks then she knows that she is happy now while he is licking and shoving his fingers and there is no shame any longer, that girl is no longer, there is the hungry girl the desirous man, the archetypal girl and boy on the floor of his workroom inside of a car at the side of roads in cheap motels (and he always pays in cash) and the blacker world becomes blacker, the fish unfished and the trees cut down and the sea is dying, he tells her, and still their yeses push out of their sticky mouths electrical and wide. I love you, she tells him, and she means: yes and now. Fuck me again, make me back into my mother a mother, today he has given her his seed and she readily awaited it, the child they could make between them if they desired and they did, he doesn't remove his seedy cock from the cunt—*in that moment* they cannot; in that moment they are themselves and not themselves. Soon, later, she drives back to her home near the bay water and she is her sons' mother again, the business woman, the polite and perhaps slightly self-righteous citizen and neighbor, an anxious girl and she is afraid, again, of? of stepping outside; she has already stepped outside with you.

She makes a stop at the pharmacy and buys the pills that they are selling; she takes them; she doesn't have a child with her lover, she is not a god now, she is modern again, she is burning gasoline when she drives the car, she is making money, thinking about the bills, thinking what she will must needs make for dinner for her boys, their homework, their grades in school, their futures and the stock exchange, politics and retirement benefits—, not of the small grey birds, not of her cunt which hums, softly, later when she puts her betraying fingers inside.

13

She dreamed of another man last night, a stranger who was falling in to love with her, beautiful and quiet and he held her hand throughout the dream. And Maman sits next to her and tells her that this is a good man, this man will love you, and not my lover, she thinks, who is my husband? and who the carpenter? And the night before, a dream she can no longer remember. Just this: that when she awoke she was happy and at ease, as if she had been visited in the night, possessed by dreaming, perhaps by the satyrs, and she realized in the dream which she then forgot that she was happy and that everything was quiet and alright and she awoke alone in her bed and alone in her house and filled too by the spirits the gods and their fluid residue; blood and aroused.

Tonight she has dinner with her husband in an expensive restaurant and she tells him that she loves him chooses him and she cries while she does it, takes bites of green salad, and she drinks her red Burgundy wine and then eats the fresh fish and cries into her fish and wine and he looks at her, shocked and terrified by the apparition in front of him, and she doesn't look into his eyes, sobs, chews, and she herself is not sure why she does it—not the phrases about loving him and saying them to him—but why it is that she is panic-driven in the nighttime, moves through the world now like a madwoman; he gets up from the table to go to the bathroom; she is becoming mad, she thinks. She is possessed by a river, or a river god, and she goes down the strong current, follows her emotions like a fish upset into the waters, she wants to be struck from the water, struck by her husband and her lover, by this river dæmon who possesses her and makes her speak in so many tongues.

14

She wonders if her heart overreaches her or is it your heart, lover, which overreaches you? Beloved, you say to her, I would like for you to spit inside my mouth and to take the breath from me, "You take my breath, empty the lung bells with your gaze, with your restraint, with your vile womanly ways. Why don't you love me enough? Why can't you, Mother, love me without restraint?"

She tells him —Listen. I have need of money. I am afraid. I don't like your stinking breath and fatty belly. I am unaroused by my lust for you. You are ugly. How is it that the beloved comes to me in your form and why is it, sir, that the quotidian destines us, like Isolde and her lover, for tragedy in the smallest and most inconsequential forms?

They take a trip together in April six months before the husband inquired about the affair. She flies home early from a business trip and meets the lover in a southern city and they rent a car and drive out toward the sea. They find a motel near the water and they go up to the room and he tells her to take of her clothes and she does it; they lie upon the bed and cannot see the sea in the distance; it is cold outside; spread your legs, he tells her, and his mouth and then all of her worries: the lies to her boss and husband and the children, the childish or violent morality to which she has been raised and to which she has strapped her stories: immaterial; and it is only the lovers again, archetypes, and his breath does not stink or her pussy belly fat look ugly in the daytime, and the snake at the base of her spine rises up slowly, tears itself out of her mouth and bites him, lovingly, on the lips.

15

They take a walk along the main avenue in the beachside town after they've made love. Almost all of the shops are closed, the fog hangs heavy on the roofs and doorways and they find and agree upon, eventually, a Greek restaurant for dinner.

Do you love me?

Yes, darling.

Will you love only me, like the one?

42

And it cannot be helped, the discourse of love is fraught with the inadequacies and fallacies of the language, and the banalities moralities of the modern industrial (American) age.

If you're like salt,
Come lie upon my wounds.

Why are you the beloved? What is it in the way that your cells your soul your heart's blood vibrate, or is it only your tongue, sir, which has made you into her god? She is prostrate for you, see her wounds, her mouth and cunt, opened, red, bloody: all of love's rivers are filled with this blood: the blood of the mother, the vaginal blood which gives itself each month and which, upon your birth, boy, your mother gave over for you also. In the blood, knowing and being, or feeling, are one and undivided...and yet, she is stuck in time and inside culture, like the moths which, drawn in, are stuck inside the glare of the electric lights inside of her home in the evenings. And this confuses her, speaks in tongues which are not the tongue you use to arouse the girl on the bed in the motel in a southern California city who has traveled the eighteen hours by airplane across the sea and mountains to find you again, you confuse her with your pedestrian looks and smells, your phrases at the airport not of the weather and the gods, but of your electric bills and the rising costs of woods and the downtrodden and your children's illnesses, piano lessons, difficulties with your wife. You are the lover? she thinks, while you are speaking on the drive to the motel. You are he? until, again and again, you tell her to take off her clothes, now you are not speaking, your tongue is making her, the winds come down, the rains, like happiness, down, she is assured, no: she is transformed again and later wonders, not at you, Lover, but at herself: she is the Beloved? Shy and terrified girl, girl with the culture's rules and decorum upon her mind like shirt sleeves on her skin.

43

16

She is in her old apartment and it is eight and a half years ago,
long before she took your tongue into her mouth and cunt
and your cock also, made a complete circuit with the blood.
She didn't know of you then, nor had she, as she does five
years later, imagined you while she sits alone in her office,
the door closed, lunchtime or late in the evening working
late, and pulls out the small vibrator she keeps in a desk
drawer and desperately imagines the man who will sit between her legs (imagines him and yet doesn't imagine that
you exist or could exist) prostrate at the altar of her sex, make
her into a god and himself and then you arrived two years
later and opened her legs in the motel on L Street and she rec-
ognized you not in your looks and not immediately either
but from sexual encounter to sexual encounter—between
her legs she recognizes, bit by bit, the man she had envi-
sioned. Perhaps I made you, she tells you, I called to you and
you arrived.

In the apartment she is forty-two weeks pregnant with her second child and she moans and labors and would like nothing more than to be outside of her form, but there is no leaving of this moment of her body and the child will come through her, will stretch the cervix wide (a mouth) and pass out from eternity and into time and culture and there is pain (there are no artificial hormones or pain relievers to take her out of it, she is present in the inward outness of the birth inside of the apartment; they do not go to hospital for this boy's birth) and when the boy passes through the cervix and begins to push out through the cunt, then the girl looks up and sees that her ancestors stand before her in a queue in the top right corner of the living room of her apartment and she recognizes her grandparents and then a group of unrecognizable men and women passing back for a thousand or ten thousand years into the wood panels and the girl knows that it is the blood that she is seeing in its human form, her maternal and paternal grandparents and then behind them the thousand others and they are smiling to see the boy coming through and passing across the threshold safely, witness the birth of the next in line: a babe with blue eyes and blue skin and then soon brown eyes and medium pale skin also. Her second boy cries and she is relieved that he is outside of her body finally.

45

17

She knows today in her body how sorrow is the lake tides, sadness rises and falls down inside of her, sweeps through the weight and stones of her organs: her thinking and blood and breathing bile organs, she feels her heart and her stomach when she sees her husband before her and he is naked and shy now to show her his form and she knows that she no longer is a guest, he takes a bath towel and covers his genitals and she doesn't suck his cock or open her anus any longer for these pleasures nor his tongue in her mouth or his look into the pupil: restrained from her, taken, pulled back and this pull, this turn away, brings up the tides like the moon's silent pull and she wonders how it is that she can feel such sadness about him today when she has gone to his house to pick up their children, just the pick up their children, the family divided, the mother and father if not enemies then not either confidants, it is this loss of confidence, she thinks, that I miss, not his cock, or his habits, his breath at night in bed, his body

46

odor and warmth in bed: she doesn't like living alone or eating alone with the children, has become accustomed to his
presence which now is the sacrifice for the gods so that the
gods could have descended inside of her form, via the cunt,
her lover the conduit.

18

They take a trip together in the summertime in the ninth
month of their affair. And the girl is anxious, she piles lie
upon lie for her children and her husband and her bosses as
to her reasons for traveling: for business for the husband and
children, for vacation for the bosses, and I will go here, and
she is instead traveling with her lover by car for a week. You
can't see any of this, you are happy that for a week you will
have the girl with you and each night you can fuck her and
each morning and you are called to her like a boy is called at
dusk by his friends on the street corners to come outside and
play, and you don't see the black mottled filth which could be
her guilt now, her fear and hoary nightsweats: and she is driving with you and the car begins to feel like a prison with you
inside of it and she would like to get outside of its windows
and steel doors and you are talking and she is not listening
but thinking of how she notices the control stops of her
breath and that you irritate her more and you are not clever
and how she doesn't like you and she doesn't love you and

she would like to return home to her husband and her children and to schedules and what she knows and to weekends
doing the laundry and dishes and her husband will fix some
things and bicycle with the boys and not this man with the
thick and scarred fingers, with the turned-out half-blind
gaze, and before you you see how your beloved becomes a
destroyer, how she is now the black night sullen girl, she
won't touch you, she speaks in monosyllables, she pulls back
mightily and down she has traveled and perhaps she has betrayed you all of this time when you thought she was the sun
and fiery blank star and she is not more than a human girl,
petty, demanding, sullen and mean today in the car in her human vicious heart.

She wants to get away from you. You stop the car at a view-
point and she walks away, tells you that she will return and
she runs down the hillside missing her husband, thinking
that she doesn't love this man, cannot wait to go home now
and feel her children's backs and thighs, their smell (and they
have five more days together in the car) and this is how we
are, she thinks, this modern nature: to want this man, your
lover, until you are spending each day with him and each
night and you don't have to leave him and then he bores
you and then he doesn't do things correctly, and then he is
not handsome or brave and you don't desire him and you
are thinking how she has become some other girl, like all
of the girls now: fickle, harsh, lying and to make the man

49

wretched—just as your own wife does as she hounds you like the meneads, eats the flesh from your bones and kills you.

And the girl wounds you, it is the first fight, the first rejection, and there will be more fights, more rejections. You don't speak on the drive to the motel. You stop for dinner at a Mexican place. She doesn't look at you, she hardly eats the food on her plate. You are sickened by her, you are angry and despairing: wasn't this the girl who would love you? Wasn't this the girl you had waited for? The one you saw at the party because of something, a radiance you called it, not her beauty, or form, but this lighted-up look looked at you and your dark woods dark moods and you wanted to hold her, suck the cunt, crawl inside the ass and thighs.

You say: I'll go home. Drop me at the airport or the bus terminal.

No, she says.

50

—I'm going out for a walk. And you leave her there in the motel and you walk for over an hour in the hot night, it is still ninety degrees at night in this city and this girl is not the girl of your dreams, she is also the devourer. She is the girl in your dreams or your crotchy imaginations. You return to the motel and she lies on the bed and she is forlorn, she looks sad and abandoned. You are angry. You take off your shoes and lie down next to her (there is no where else to put the body).

Listen, you say.

And you will talk with her for hours and then you will take off your clothes and she removes her clothes also. You are fucking and then you fall asleep. When you awaken you resume your journey with the girl, the beloved, she is chagrined she is impatient, you take her hand and she drives the car towards your destination.

19

Her face has changed in the past eighteen months: she is older and also younger looking. People tell her she looks younger and she looks at her face in the mirror and she knows that there are many more lines in her forehead and around her eyes and mouth; her face has become elongated and stretched across the bones around her eyes and cheeks from weight loss and perhaps it is just age, she thinks, she knows it is sorrow and fear and then the orgasms to pull out the veins like a triptych in the middle of her brow; the orgasms which give the vitality, the fear, its untoward companion, what makes the grooves in her aging face. Soon I won't be beautiful any longer and men will not look at me as they do now; you are beautiful, he tells her, pretty girl, good girl, let me suck your cunt.

She doesn't tell him until weeks after their first meeting, or months, how she had sought other lovers before him, that he was not her first unhusbandly cock (nor likely the last, she doesn't say it but he, in his knowing way, knows it) and it is

52

then that he demands that she fuck only him, I don't want you to fuck your husband anymore, he tells her, and she looks at him in disgust and arousal, knows that this is possession, knows in her thoughts what she has long known in her body, it has been her body which has brought her to this man, the cunt itself, calling out into the air and seeking the lover who could lay her back, remove her underpants, and push his mouth and nose into the hairy sex, that her body demanded it, sent out the signs or vibrations, the scent of her, of this woman who needed to know and to know only by having the experience, which is, after all, the source of all knowledge—the body itself: the penis and its desires to be enveloped, the cunt which wants the cock for itself: the circle of the two energies, the union each seeks and hardly finds in this city and time. And she must have known when she encountered him for the first time at the business party and he was there by pure chance, as a favor to a friend to keep him company, and they were introduced and he tells her of his woods and boxes and long dark mahogany chests and she doesn't think him handsome or attractive, but there is a hum between them like the sounds a machine makes when it moves in synch to complete its work-arc and the force passes between them and invisible like sounds are invisible and he gives her his number so that if she is interested in the boxes, cabinets and chests for her home she can call him like he has invisibly called out to her tonight. She calls him in ten days, and she has never initiated a call to a lover before, seeks him out, agrees to meet with him at a pub downtown in her city

53

and he will bring the portfolio of his work. He tells her that he is driving to her city on business and he will be able to meet her in the evening, on whichever day she would like, and she tells him Tuesday and six PM, and she walks into the bar and she is wondering if she will remember what he looks like, and later he tells her how the business had not been the business of his woods, but how he had wanted to see her, how he had known immediately who she was (for him), how her cunt called to him and he was familiar with electric currents and so he came for her and made the excuse of business and sat in the pub for hours before the six o'clock meeting time, at the front of the bar so that he wouldn't miss her arrival, drinking beer after beer.

There are many things she can say to her lover in the first weeks of their affair that she cannot say to him later and that she can never communicate to the husband, that can be said when one is known only sexually and without the habits and interceding fears of the conventional self and before the roles are set and the patterns established, when it is only the vibrations of the man and the vibrations of the woman, then everything is seeable in its nature, the essences emerge, each man and each woman is an icon, an idol, and her large brown eyes call to him and she is his muse, he tells her, I'll make woods into glories; and she tells him how he is a sad man, a beautiful man, she can see that he is a man who needs love like a small boy left out of the mother's bosom: I can love you, she tells him, let me love you without limits and before she loves him she recognizes his tribe of men, the poets who have gone alone singing their suffering, playing the lyre, seeking the girls who will tear them to pieces and make them back into their sons and lovers; I'll do it for you, she says, let me love you, she tells him, long before she loves him she feels this desire to love him, the god in him, and the god in her before their usual selves make themselves felt and they argue about the days and the political campaigns or how to make this thing and that one or simply that he doesn't phone her everyday or that she thinks that he is cheap with his money and doesn't buy her small gifts or expensive dinners. But in bed the gods descend again and he is a thousand years old and she is his night and the darkness makes them into eternal lovers and everything is right and good and joy moves from her form out into the night skies stars which she doesn't see in her city and back again as light moves.

This then what she doesn't understand, how this man who takes her form and reforms her, pleasures her, takes her out and makes her feel that she is alive now and while she lies with him afterwards in the bed she falls asleep like a small child in the late afternoon, the sun does not enter their lair, there are no windows, the sounds of trucks and motorcycles can be heard outside of the thin walls, a building is demolished next door and the sound of broken-up concrete and jack hammers and contented and unaware that she has descended into sleep until she awakens and her head is resting on his shoulder and her arm is on his soft belly and he is looking at the ceiling and at her, I slept, she tells him, and he is silent, I am contented, she tells him, and then at some moment in their late and unsunlighted afternoon in his workroom, the sadness will come down upon her as it always does, the old companion, for she has always been the sad girl, quiet at the side of rooms and behind the tables and her maman's skirts, she doesn't speak to adults when she is a child or to strange men now, and the sadness is with her now as it is with him, and later he will admit to her that he has always desired the sad girls, that he is drawn to them as if to a particular scent or shape of a girl's breast or thigh, or the way that she looked at him from across the table that day on their second meeting in the Japanese restaurant.

20

They fight regularly now. She waits in anticipation every day for his call on the telephone, he must call her if he loves her and she waits somewhat impatiently for the ringing device, will not pick up for anyone else but him, ignores her husband's and mother's attempts to reach her —I am working hard, she tells everyone, when they ask why it is that she never picks up the phone. And she waits for him, waits in the recesses of her mind for him, stores up all of the things that she will say to him, stores up her sore doubts and fears, her loneliness which she will then push into her voice, she thinks, and she will tell him of her day, of her son's broken tooth, of her desire to spread her legs for him today and again and she can't bear the six day wait until she sees him and the blue marks on her neck are idled over like jewelry and then it is ringing and she knows it is him and she answers and he says hello darling and then there it is again, inexplicable to the girl herself who waited in anticipation and lust and lovingness—the wave down of sadness, of cold resentment, she feels suddenly cold and she has nothing to say to him; hello fine yourself?; and: I am very busy with work. And he tries to draw her out, he was so happy when he phoned and then in moments his voice also falls down into a sort of trial and fatigue and he can't understand how his beloved has become this sullen girl who only gives him the monosyllabic reply and so he can't wait to get off of the phone and resume his carvings—the woods always generous and responsive—and they hang the phone and the girl has sunk into despair and now hates her lover, and herself, and thinks of killing herself and again of the car on the highway and how she will swerve into traffic and snap out of it, she chides herself, what is your problem? And like one cannot fathom the gods, she also cannot fathom herself in love or why it is that with her lover the quiet dark and despairing parts of herself emerge, would like him to possess her and hold himself to her; she demands the boy's sacrifice; cannot bear to love him and wishes only to love him on his unsunlighted bed with the sounds of break-ing concrete and machinery and trucks and motorcycles to accompany their lovemaking in the hot valley afternoons.

58

We know everything, he tells her, she has her back to him now in bed, she is angry with him, abhors him and herself, wonders that she has ever taken the risk to drive this long dis-tance, the lies she tells each day to her husband and boss, the marks she hides under her clothes—his hands' and mouth's —she closed her legs to her husband as she was directed by her god, and he is petty and does not tell her that he loves her every day, and she wants those words during each exchange and demented if he won't give them, if you love me then tell me it and he tells her that she knows, she knows it all, she knows that she and her husband were finished a long time back; she knows that Americans walk the earth like tiny sad half-blinded animals, as if a new species out of one of Scheherazade's stories in The Thousand Nights and One Night, a species which won't see or know, which puts a limit on all things: love and desire and how to feel and how to fuck and each person wears his mask voluntarily: what stops people from peeking behind the mask and seeking the is, the moment, the life as it swarms spills hovers and recovers itself: is there any where on earth as lonely as this country? he asks her and he tells her (he continually reminds her that he is not American) that we know everything, but we don't wish to look at it, especially here, here people live in their self-made tunnels, their eyes covered by cultural mores membranes, like technological steel moles.

21

Last night she dreamed about you. And in this dream you
don't look like yourself, your hair is dark and you are thinner
and you are both in another city in the dream, it could be Los
Angeles, and you are walking near the 405 Freeway on the
west side of the city near the old Veterans Hospital, which,
she thinks, is now something else and not what it was in the
years she used to drive by there with her father on the drive
to her grandmother's house when she was a girl. And the
other side of the freeway is a ravine and down the dirt ravine
they are in Mexico and then Guatemala, and here in this small
shanty and dirty roaded town everyone is dressed in the tra-
ditional huipil and the Indian ladies look at her as if to let her
know that she doesn't understand, and she doesn't, she realizes, understand how it would be to live outside of American
morality which asks that all things be sacrificed not to the
gods, but to commerce and the anxiety of what could be,
what might happen, *for safety*, the ladies in her children's class-
rooms murmur, and the dark-haired costumed woman in
her dream points to the naked Indian child and the naked-

ness is beautiful and does not invite the lewd hand, for lewd-
ness is also a product of her father's culture (the dirty body,
sex is dirty) and in theirs the days are marked differently,
two calendars to mark the days and the body is not reviled.
And her lover asks her to travel with him to Venezuela in the
dream, but I don't have any money, she says, and now she realizes as the story is passed into sentences, that if she wants
to she can travel to Venezuela and out of the United States, if
she wants to she doesn't have to partake of this Protestant
modern theatre and its roles, that she can, she is a woman and
the vibrations are real, pull back and pull open the labia of
her cunt, invite the world, her lover, inside and do less, un-
worry the world, sit and listen to this story while it is told.

22

And so he returns again from another trip abroad. This time he has gone to sell his boxes and trunks in the north of Europe and to purchase woods there, see the skies and brush of birds in the morning fields; he has drunk their liquors and eaten the fish and tells her, upon his return, how much he liked the fjords and wind.

She picks him up at the airport. She drives the long drive over the hills and now the late summer grasses are completely desiccated and most of the wild flowers have died alongside the freeway and she drives quickly, 90 miles per hour, for she is late as usual, has left her children with her nephew, and drives to get him, looks in the rearview mirror constantly for the lurking policemen who have ticketed her already two times on these trips south and arrives at the airport and doesn't see him waiting for her, and she wonders if she does want to see him or perhaps she has tired of him, she thinks, that their love wanes with distance and her moods and she parks the car and walks into the airport terminal and sees him by the luggage carousel and he looks anxious is looking around for her and has a week's growth of beard and his eyes red with fatigue and he sees her then, he looks happy and relieved, perhaps he worried that she wouldn't arrive for him, that she would have forgotten him, and opens his arms to her, doesn't kiss her lips, tells her that he has been ill for the past week and says to the man standing next to him that this is his girl, she smiles at the stranger that he has met on the flight from New York.

Two nights later when she is alone again and in bed and her children are asleep in the next room and she is falling into sleep, almost unconscious, she will suddenly awaken fully and realize that she has three or four men like icons in her mind, and that today or yesterday when she spent the day with the returned lover—who in her conscious mind has been her adulterous short-term affair lover—he had already merged with an older archetype, the man in the grey area of herself that she is only vaguely aware of: who will possess her, whom she possesses, sucks his fat cock, takes his seed, rides him without the boundaries of polite American society, without its self-consciousness: that there have been three (or four) images, three (or four) men, men's faces: her father her school professor her first boyfriend husband and now her lover joins the company of men in her mind, merges with them into the old one, the god-man, so that when he fucks her and she can only open her legs wider and she wants more and more and he is fatigued from the long transatlantic flight and cannot fuck her as she needs to be fucked, she is begging him and stretching her thigh muscles taut and this opening he has made in her makes her want to carry him always in her cunt: she is at home now only when he sticks it in her, rides her, fills her up, then she is lovely, he is lovely, the world is right, she is at ease, and knows to what for what she was born.

23

Last night, weeks later, in your workroom in your bed she dreamed of the sea. And then she was in a cave or bunker by the sea and the waves rushed in and you were with a group of friends, or perhaps you were not in her dream at all: the waves crested high and wide and terrifying above her head and she thought that she would drown there in her dream and she remembered inside of the dream how it was when she was a girl in Los Angeles and in the warm waters of southern Mexico and she would go to the sea with her parents and they would swim and waggle their fingers and legs and in Los Angeles she waded into the surf and many times the waves crashed down upon her head and burying her in the white water and hitting her girl's body against the brown and crushed glass rocks sand, she would be tossed about and think that she were going to die then, suffocated by the white and green giant which held her to the earth and would not release her for the duration of the waves roiling. And in her dream she is terrified like the eight-year-old girl in the Pacific Ocean was and by herself, her parents a distant mark on the

dry and hot sand sunning themselves. And when she awakens she thinks about her terror and your sex and how when
you make love the world crashes also and she will die perhaps and wild love, of wideness . . . She has come to love you
desperately: your wide blue look; your soft belly and fat legs;
your feet splayed and the gait of the body as it approaches
her, you wave an arm high in the crowd to signal to her that
you have seen her, that she is the center which calls to you,
the wink of the eye so that she knows again and again and
she knows it in the dark last night in bed when you have
sucked and licked and played with her cunt—and she has
flown off into sleep, flown into the dream of the sea and
inside the dream the memory of childhood when she was
alone there and terrified as she is terrified when she awakens
that this man, you, take her off and down into the depths
death where she is would only like to, must needs to, return:
again and again.

24

Now you have departed again (and again): you have left for three weeks to do business in another country; to buy the woods; to carve them; to make the boxes furniture tables and bookshelves with the woods of Indonesia, West Africa, New Zealand and she is lonely. She misses you; she would like nothing better than to lie in your arms naked and the world passes by the lovers outside of their small estate and you put your hand in her cunt and you don't speak and slowly you begin to rub against the clitoris and she notices her breath notices how she is not sure that she can come that she loves you and your eyes close and rubbing stinging her clitoris and putting two and three fingers inside of her sex and she splays her legs for you, widely, looks at the photographs and paintings on the wall of your workroom and which she has now memorized: the faces of the girls and men in the photographs hanging there (they look like ecstasy); and: she loves you like she has never loved her husband; or any man; and it is impossible that you will live and love together: her children your children your wife and the other impediments to

67

love and lovers; and why not? she thinks: you are the soul's mate and a beloved from the good or bad love-poems and the great men of poetry who write of their muses of their Lauras: and when you are together and naked then all of your human ancestry speaks in your cock and cunt; culture and caste is obliterated and made fine: a man; a woman: and in love, loving each other timelessly, across time and culture and his cock in her cunt and she is happy and he is happy to have stuck it in her: a man and in woman: open: the communion the old books spoke of.

She has received a phone call from you today and you tell her about your travels and the people who welcome you into their homes and businesses and the drinks you have and the foreign foods and I love you, you tell her when she picks up the phone when you call, before she has a chance to speak, simply her Hello? and then I love, darling, and she is put at ease and you know that she is an uneasy girl, anxious girl, who is not sure that you love her, enough, that it is right with you; she herself unsure as to why it is then when you are not with her that she panics, like a small child, and thinks that you don't love her, that you don't exist even, that the lover is some idea she made up from some, a romance, she read once or many times and you could not have arrived and you could not have made her into this other woman, the woman who lives in your arms in your workroom below the hanging photographs of men and women from other countries that you have taken on your many travels abroad. She re-reads the

letter you have left her. Don't read it, you tell her, until I depart, and so she leaves you at the airport and rushes home to
open the missive. Is it inside of the letter, she wonders. This,
what?—proof, she thinks. That he is right; that he is the man
who makes unmakes her; that? Again the anxious American
girl always seeks the outcomes; the future. I am not from
here, he reminds her when he is about to leave; I have no need
to contain my longings and fears behind false wickets.

He calls again today and he is calling each day, knows that she
needs the calls from the ether and she asks him, after the requisite exchanges of pleasantries things-to-do things he she
has dones: do you love me still? She is embarrassed and shy
and yet it pushes out of her: still? as before? and it is not the
reassurances that you give her: of course, darlings; yeses; but
the sound of your breath after the question is made, a certain
hitch in it, a pulled up and released and she hears in your
breath, in this hiccup of air (and the words don't matter) she
knows that you have fallen more in love with her, that these
eighteen months have made you more her lover, and that,
against the vagaries of reason and what ought to be done, you
have fallen and remain deeply in love with a girl who is distant from you and who you have taught to spread her legs out
nightly widely for the wildness in her and in you also.

25

She takes her children to the local beach and they play happily in the low surf and in the sand for hours and she had long ago gotten used to their needs of her, their mamas called out in a constant refrain, but today her children are contented and she begins to feel bored in the heat and sun and wishes she had brought a book to read or her computer to continue her business work and so scans the beach for some kind of entertainment and gets caught up in the gaggle of girls adjacent to her, the twelve-year-old nymphs in their skinny legged bodies and taught thighs and pulled back into ponytails hair, and they are playing with a volleyball in a circle to her right and every so often the ball hits close to her and she is irritated and she hears them, these unfucked girls, chatting and cheering each other on about the handsome older boys a few hundred feet away and they are yelling that *he is so hot!* And these girls are heated and no wonder the boys want to stick it into them and they seemingly, awkwardly, unaware of their power, and yet their urges, at twelve, rush around the beach like fired invisible rockets. Her children still do not know this sex drive, but they will soon enough, she knows, as she herself did, an awkward girl who needed to be fucked and who wanted the boys and who, awkward, shy, and fat, turned from the boys and the boys turned from her and who did not get fucked until eighteen. What would my life have been like if I had been beautifully and lovingly and regularly fucked from the age of twelve when I began to need it so badly, like these girls? she thinks.

The desire to merge, so obvious when we know without knowing that all of it—this knowing—comes from the body and that the ideas phenomena represent it to us and we made from our father's seed and our mother's ovum inside of the mother's cunt: this to merge: we beings of the cosmic merger and long for a return, then, like abandoned shells in the Paleozoic seas . . . to the mother? Or to that first primordial moment, the electric being, when the spermatozoon is taken and aroused into the egg and the immediate vibrations electric of our coming into being. She realizes it, even though she knows, when she is talking to her son and telling him how it is that he was made, of the reproductive organs penis vagina and —Yuch, he says to her, and laughs, and she laughs also.

71

26

Today you are not here again and then again and she is lonely, as usual, and decides between the glasses of wine, she is alone and her children are with her husband, that she will go to the cinema and watch a love story. And she goes and perhaps you call her on the telephone from Europe while she is watching the film and tell her how happy you are and how much you love her and that she is like a small and blue butterfly and she listens to your message while she drives home; she sobs while she drives; drives slowly with her sobs for accompaniment. She is not certain, even, why it is that she is sobbing: for the missed phone call and that she cannot reach you, or simply that she feels her ancient sorrow in her bones and now lungs; or she is tired and without her children's laughter and distractions and games and requirements, realizes that she feels pitiful, pitiable; she feels sorry for herself and that her lover is married to another woman and that her lover is traveling in Europe with his family and that her lover is not here with her today and by her side and opening her legs and opening her soul out to the universe.

27

She takes a walk with the husband. He is polite and he is civilized and they don't say to one another what it is or was that caused such anguish between them. She looks at him and she is anguished. And she can never tell him what it is or why it is that they are no longer lovers, that he couldn't summon her soul in a dark or undark night. Why she had to seek it outside of the marriage, how she was desperate for it: to live, to have a cock in her cunt taking her out, apart; a man prostrate between her legs and adoring her for eternity or the night today.

keeps raining all the time

You are still traveling and you will be gone for the remainder of the summer. Your daughters travel with you and you are happy to be out of the country and looking at woods and with your daughters and although you will fight with your wife during the two weeks that she is with you, you are, in large part, contented: working on what you love and your daughters by your side as they chatter and travel the railways and eat the foreign foods. And you do love the girl you've left behind in California and she has begun dreaming about you every night and it is the same dream: she is in her childhood neighborhood and she is with her friends whom she cannot recall upon waking and in last night's dream the friend tells her, who is a co-worker, who is her lover, that he doesn't love her, that he has in fact, all of this time, been fucking his wife and ex-girlfriends; that his love is a facsimile of love, American-style, and she is walking home toward her childhood home in the dream, she walked those streets every day in summer as a girl and often alone and she thinks, upon waking, that she is always alone in her dreams as she felt in childhood and that this is the dream she keeps dreaming all of the time and each man, her husband, her first boyfriend, her old college boyfriends, you, fall into her dreams and into the dream lover who doesn't, in the dream, ever love her enough, who leaves her and of course they all belong to her father, that old man in the dreams who is behind the faces of all of her lovers and you call her from Antwerp and tell her that you

love her and she is crying, hysterically, would like to tell you about her dream but there is no time for it and then you hang up and when the phone is disconnected she has the sick feeling in her stomach that she often gets with you, and with you only, she is love-sick and the only way out of it is your form itself and you between her legs and your sweat and piss and semen spread across her thighs.

You called her this evening and so the calls accumulate in this book. And she is telling you about her work and projects and she is happy today, today she doesn't think that she cannot bear it, bear the absence of your body and to lie in your arms so that she will be at ease. One more week until you return, she tells herself, and goes through the motions of the day. And only once or twice today as she was not looking in the corner of things, did she sense that goblin on the ledge, her lodged friend, old although not dear companion which is this despair has long been hers, winked back in his glassy manner, grey matter, monster.

She has driven to see you for you have returned. And you open the door to your workroom and say how are you and she begins, at that moment, to leave you. She goes down into sorrow and she can't say it is because you are not here, because in fact you have returned, and you leave together and drive into the mountains to spend three days together. And now you are together in a small hotel high in the Sierra Nevada and she sees the snow on the mountain peaks from the window and the wind catches in the poplars and pine and small children linger on the streets and run to find their balls and bicycles and you have fucked her four times already and she is not sure why, but when you fuck her she is not very aroused, her cunt is dry and so you lick your fingers and wipe them inside her cunt, put your penis inside of her and heave onto her body and she thinks that she is happy you are inside of her and pushing against her, but she does not take off with you, she herself cannot say why—whence the sadness? And two days later you are driving back to your city and she thinks that it has been in error, that your love is no more than a small and god-like error, and that the man she left behind with the children has made her life livable and that with you she is undone and she is too afraid, for the undoneness, for the aloneness which descends now when you are not with her, if you don't call her, when you don't gaze at her with more than cursory recognition or a hello. The possession has come down the river to take her to a town in the mountains and the music plays in the background and without reason she leaves the hotel room on the night you arrive into the mountains and you are watching the television or reading your magazines on the woods and trends in furniture and she is crying and she has no idea why it is that she sits in the car for fifteen minutes after she tells you that she is going to seek something in the car and cries as if she is a child and a mean girlfriend has abandoned her on the tarmac playground, or her mother at school when she was four or five years old, and you have not, you sit waiting for her in the room, but she cannot understand it, does not understand her own impulses and urges or why it is that the man she has pined for for weeks like a small girl now makes her cry, slowly and quietly, in the backseat of the car high in the mountains with the pines and grey-green poplars whistling the winds like a chorus of wood instruments.

And she thinks how she doesn't understand herself or whom she loves or why or the motives for it—this urge which has pushed her up into your workroom and pulled you down between her legs and she panics, that she has abandoned her husband their home and the family edifice for the shy seeking stubborn and half-blind man who licks her cunt without speech. Has it been in error? And if so, which error has it been? She has lunch with her husband, the tall and solemn man with the dark brown eyes and he tells her that he is thinking to divorce her, that things are not working out, that she has caused him a pain without surcease, that she betrays him each time that she drives south to see her lover in the desiccate valley with summer-burned grasses and scattered oak trees. He has discovered her lies, he says, he knows that she has driven with her lover to the mountains and that that man has pushed his cock into her cunt and that she was pleasured by him and has, again, betrayed their vows, her cunt wide open, her mouth also, for the lover's tongue. And while he says all of this to her, she is drinking a glass of cold white wine and sees the maple across the street and how its leaves move like small dancers scattered across the thousand small branches and she is crying silently and then she is sobbing, silently, in the small corner restaurant which gives onto the busy streets of the city and the maple across the way. And she tells her husband that she still loves him, that she has always loved him and cannot tell him what it is inside of her that made her seek her lover and lie with and then lie to the

brown-eyed man before her, again and again, cause such a
well of pain and she doesn't see it now, with his dark and
mean phrases, but suddenly, like a wind inside of her, a ca-
cophony of woods, feels him come down into her, feels his
sorrow like a winded heft, a high-arched dark stone cathe-
dral and she is sorry, she says, for his sorrow, feels it, for all
that she has caused him, that (why couldn't he love her more?
adore her cunt? Know that she needed him to and to lick her
and suck the clitoris and make her into another woman, an
ancient girl at the side of the river or beneath the green-grey
poplars and the cosmos on a clear and still mountain night
and her soul ascends, the outness arrives and she could never
ask it of him (her old shame) but the lover knew without
speech and without asking and on their trip into the mountains he opens her legs in the middle of the night while she
is sleeping, holds her, pushes his cock into her guilty dry
cunt. And even with her desiccate and moral cunt, she was
happy to have him inside of her) she wishes she had not.

78

28

Last night she dreamed of ghosts in her childhood home. She returns home in her dream to the suburban ranchhouse she was raised in and where the mice invaded the kitchen drawers and her father in a rage pulled her mother by her hair down the long dark hallway and then later another man pushed a window open in the dining room and entered their home and raped her younger sister while the others in the house remained asleep. In her dream she is sitting on the floor of the yellow kitchen and she has her dog with her, although the dog is not the black and white bitch of her childhood, but her own children's dog, the young black terrier and she holds the black dog close in the yellow kitchen and she is afraid, because she knows that there are ghosts in the house, just as she knew it as a child and that now in her adult dream in the yellow mice-infested kitchen, she will see them, she will not be able to run down the long dark hallway and hide from them, or her father, or the invisible man who stalked her mother at a bar and followed her home in his car and broke a window and entered their home and fucked her sister late in the night. To her dog she whispers that they are alone in the house, sees a light in the corner of her eye, a white blinking luminescent jewel, gets up and goes into the bathroom and sees that the toilet is filled with shit and toilet paper. She flushes the toilet and the shit and paper and water run over the bowl and onto the bathroom floor and begin to flood the house. When she wakes, she is alone in her adult house and it is quiet because the children are with her husband who will, eventually, not be her husband and she thinks that she is depressed or lonely or sad and scared, like a girl, she thinks, I am again that quiet and afraid girl in the closet of the mice-infested house on Grove Street.

29

The girl without speech doesn't read this book to her husband or her lover. She is traveling again and alone for business and now sits in an airport in an American city, she is tired, she drinks a coffee, she eats a sandwich and cookie. Now I will decide, she thinks, who it is that I love, which man is my mate and she laughs at her own girlishness, the girl who read romance novels (like her foreign mother), the girl who thinks that a man is a christ and saves her, not from the barbarian hordes at the borders, but from the devils within her own form, which plague her, which pull her down, which devour her, eat her blood her vital organs, sicken and kill her. This is anxiety, she says, as if reading a school textbook. This is fear. She invites a psychoanalyst into the room to interrogate what it is that she feels, pass his judgment, correct her and make her back into the good woman, good mother, good citizen for the nation.

She rings you and you don't answer; or your wife answers; she can't reach you. She calls you again; tomorrow; and she can't reach you. Your wife says that she will pass on the message to you. The girl thinks that she would like to kill herself; that she can't reach you. Later, when she is no longer despairing she will wonder at that despairing and dramatic girl, the girl who wanted to hurt you with knives and her words and her body, if she could, when she couldn't find you, speak with you, on all of the blue-black days.

Today she wakes up in the morning and she woke up also in the middle of the night and knows or thinks that she knows that it has all been misaligned and that this man, her lover, does not save her, she has descended again into the dark place where neither her husband nor her lover are allowed entry or where the girl, a woman but it is always the girl who makes the journey beneath the stairwell beneath the wooden patio inside of the closet behind her mother's skirt down the well, is alone and broods and cries, and she herself doesn't know why she does it, why she is the sad girl, the girl who, alone now in the living room of her large and empty home, sits here, the pathetic and snot-covered face, spits into her hands, cries into her house's silence, regrets that she is this girl today, as she has always been, lonelier than the mountain gods and her children are not at home and she turns on the television to hear the blare of the plastic screened faces and some noise, some false phrases as a comfort in the late night tonight.

82

30

She has taken her children and she has left the city for the weekend. She is tired, she thinks, of this perpetual anguish, which is the illusions the stories she makes in her head, has made since she was the girl beneath the wooden deck of her childhood home. See the girl suffer, and she laughs as her children jump into the swimming pool in the hot northeastern countryside where she has brought them. She reads a book while they are swimming and she wears sunglasses and a large hat and her children are playing *Marco Polo* and soon they will be too old for these games and the beauty of their bodies and their openness, even now, pleases her, reminds her of how they sucked her breasts as small and mewling screaming babes, how they awakened her night after night for years and each morning, early, earlier than she could bear, to then bring her to this moment when she is filled full as if of mother's milk, of this love for them of their forms, their sweated smells, their tiring and bickering, their calls of Mama, even today in the swimming pool of the house they have traveled to for the long summer weekend.

She sees a red-tailed hawk above the hills of the valley and the olive trees planted by her friend in her friend's garden and farther on the scrub and the browns of the dry heated land and the rectangles of vine plantings in the far-off distance and a white car which comes up the dirt road towards this side of the hill and the grey-brown horizon, the air hangs like a shroud, her children holler and laugh and splash like small children and she is happy reading a book about a boy in southern Africa who wants to get fucked every lonely day at his school in the veldt. The three of them are together today, along with the boy in the book, and she is happy, for the moment, and thinks how happiness is found in the brown red-tipped hawk above her, in the wide grey-brown sky, in a stretched view without cars except the one which arrives to its owner's adjacent lot, and the noise of the city and its oppressive requirements, its to-do's and bills and a heart which collapses under the modern's requirements and desiccate and possessed and anxious and, rather, obsessed with her ideas (from where?) of what life is; lonely; and today she is happy with the hawk, the olive trees, muted sunlight, a wide view of hills, with an openness inside of her, some kind of lifted heft, lifted flight, and the joy of this early afternoon light.

She thinks that they will come to an end soon, or later. She isn't thinking it while they drive to his workroom, or while he takes off her clothes or while, naked, she has no trouble no shame, spreads her thighs opens her cunt lips wide with her fingers, shoves her cunt up to his mouth and happily, she is open now, she is happy, although an hour later she sobs on the floor of his workroom and tells him that she knows that he won't love her that he will not leave his wife that she is lonely on the nights without her children that she wants to die now that why doesn't he save her that why doesn't he love her enough to do it? that Will you marry me, he asks her. And she says she won't; cries it to him; cries uncontrollably on the drive northward to her home, quiet and clean, and he is home with his daughters and wife and unhappy at home, but in company, in form, in his marriage of seventeen years.

What does it mean to know something when what we know has traveled off farther out into the distance of this afternoon lighted sky and the hawk knows it, her children might still re-member in their childish memories, that the light, the earth's vibrations, the gods and is is all that matters, all there may be.

She thinks that now she is becoming his harridan, or a ban-shee, she wails outside the windows of time (alongside the defeated dead). She is becoming such a mythical and ser-pent-headed creature, who, bitter, dark, devouring, would like to kill her lover, devour his cock, kill him when he makes her suffer, and, how he makes her suffer, and she makes you suffer now, loves to see you cry in the dark and then to make you run toward her anxiously, fear that now, or now, that she will leave you alone and you will be alone forever, married and alone as you have long been, since you were that quiet and suffering child, a boy in a house filled with skeletons.

So now when she hears his voice the descent begins inside of her. She can't stop it; she does not know why it is, there is no cause of it, only the chemical feeling, a rush down, like a waterway moving through her form: misery's pitiful river and her suffering is her own and now even when he fucks her it is there, the clawed beast, feral, dangerous and devours him then her. "Should I let you go?" you ask her; I don't make you happy anymore. And she is screaming into his ears: fuck you fuck you fuck you and please make me come; please. No, she says, but you must be mine now, or. "Or?" Or I will leave you, I will fuck other men; I will kill myself you and I can't bear it: I am alone and. And. And. "No," you say, "no."

31

She dreamed of snakes last night. She was not with her lover in the dream, but with another man, a young man, a blond with blue eyes, she has seen him at her office, she has lunched with him and her bosses, he smiles brightly, he mischievously laughs when the girls bend down. She and the blond are on a motorcycle together and they are driving across town. She is not in a recognizable town, there are bridges and waterways, she could be in Europe, she is not sure. Then they are together and moving faster and faster and she is driving and he is behind her and whispering in her ear and she is telling him that they are moving too fast and she is afraid and she sees the snakes, fat and thin, long and longer, and they are driving over them for miles and he tells her that they are safe, that they do not bite, that they will not bite her naked ankles as they move through them, they are not a poisonous variety. She is comforted by what he knows and then they are driving down a hill and picking up speed and faster again and afraid she puts her naked feet onto the asphalt to slow the machine, drags her feet along, worries about the pain, about tearing them, ruining them, but she must slow it down, she thinks, they will crash otherwise, they will lose control of the machine.

32

She has spoken on the phone with the husband and he is distant, cold, he dislikes her now, he loathes her, it is the revulsion of the cuckold, a dear hatred, painfully earned, he holds himself off from her, even his voice will not ease into her ear, I'll not love you again, he doesn't say it or think it, speaks in that distant American manner, did you attend to the children's needs? Did you pay (*such and such*) bill? Must I still give money to the bitch who opened her legs as if in heat and breaking thereby the rules the vows the agreement and then *you broke my heart*. She would like you back, she thinks, come back to me and we'll make a home like two small children building a play-house and fill it with toys and children and happiness. I am lonely. Weren't we happier together? And she marvels now, at herself, at the space that her imagination fills in on the phone when he is not around to make happiness and wholeness from the edges of old desires and fears like unopened boxes.

And she is thinking of how she knows nothing (everything) about love. She thinks that she would like to reunite with the husband, that she hates her lover, that she would like to fuck the young and beautiful blond man at her office, his gaze into her, her cunt fills and vibrates when he comes nearer; she is forgetting her lover she is forgetting her husband she is crying she is lonely she would like to reunite with the husband she would like to marry the lover, she wants only to fuck the man from her office and there is another man, the black, and he laughs into her throat and she wants to open her cunt wide for him, dreams of kissing him, tells a story to herself of their love affair on the coast of northwestern Spain.

She doesn't love you any longer. She is quiet in the room with you. She thinks that you smell badly; that you are too fat; she is unattracted. She takes off her clothes in the hotel room. Let me eat your cunt, you say. She lies down on the bed. She is unenthusiastic. Without mystery. She is thinking of her bills, or her mortgage, of time; she thinks about her husband and his bony long beautiful feet. You put your mouth to her cunt. Your mouth and her cunt are in relation, in a relationship. The girl knows it, knows it again while you are kissing her cunt lips. Her cunt loves you. Her cunt knows more than she knows, than she is able to know. In love. Or perhaps the cunt is crazy; or she is. She loves you. She hates you. Mania.

33

When she thinks of the husband she feels grief. She tries not
to think of him. Of his feet and legs and of his tenderness or
small habits (the beloved ones). She will try and think of his
unbeloved habits; how he didn't desire her; would not fuck
her; how he had disappeared into some kind of white chry-
salis, a place where good workers and polite citizens resided.
How he didn't look at her; could not?: would not see her, as
she was: fat lusty hungry. Hungry for what she didn't know
of, as children are often unable to name the source of their
fears, but feel afraid, feel aggrieved, or anxious: they are crying in their mothers' arms at the end of the school day or at
the beginning of the day, they rail outside the classroom
door, for what they are unable to say, but the sobbing is real
and her hunger was real, and he didn't desire to sit at the altar of her cunt and she too ashamed, a proper girl, to beg him
to do it.

Of course she loves him. She has loved him since she was a
young woman, the college girl inside of awkward bright

91

days. And he was bright also and showed her his back his legs his neck where it is soft and liked to be sucked and pressed.

How the girl suffers with the lover with the husband. She loves the one she loves the other; she hates the one she is indifferent to the other. She would like answers like she wanted solutions to fall out neatly onto her paper and into her mathematics teacher's loving and cruel corrective hands.

Everything she knows, thinks (your mouth pressed against the cunt) she knows with her cunt. Other knowledge is a facsimile, or falling away, like the first and demised races, the mythic clay and wood men, who battered and who broken into pieces of themselves, or analyzed like book commentary in clean and clean-smelling unpissed classroom exercises.

They are together. He sits alone now among his woodpiles and she broods in another room. Why don't you fuck me? or: Why don't you love me? or: Why do you fuck me so much? or: Why do you love me as much? She picks her nose while he cannot see her; she eats her own mucus. She eats from her cunt, wipes her secretions onto her upper lip, to smell herself, love herself, eat her own body each day. She sticks her finger into her asshole. The asshole itches and she washes her hands, removes the shit, she is lonely she is tired of her lover, she doesn't like him, she loves him, she cannot live without him, she would like other lovers. She desires to return to her husband, she fears being alone, she wants more children, she would like to be free; the lover annoys; he smells; he tells her this and that and what she ought to be doing. She is childish with him, mean and spits into his food. She hates him. She is an orphan. She loves him; she likes to suck his cock for days.

Then when the husband arrives, he is chagrined, he is no longer angry, his love for her has burnt down to a small and almost invisible blue pyre and although he loves, he won't love her any longer and tells her that he felt constrained, and he says it as if the word itself pulled his limbs his mind backwards and tied and burnt him. You don't love me? she says. He says—What is love. And then she senses that it has not been love which has defeated them and she is not sure what came in to do it, wrest them out of each other, her own urges, perhaps, outside of the moral codes and fear and she hurt the husband, the girl with the wild red black lipped cunt; she destroyed him with her ways with her lies with her spread open and voracious tonguéd vaginal lips.

93

I stop, he says; I stopped. He is tight. He is sad and tight. His shoes tied, his shirt tucked; she loves him, she thinks, she cries when he closes the front door, she grieves for the husband the father of her sons: he has held her, he gave his seed for their loud crying laughing boys. Maudlin and stupid bitch. She still, she is, she would like yet this yes: to be a yes.

Her vaginal lips are engorged, red and darker red and now, after her orgasm and inside of its last vestigial thrum, she can know things, she feels knowledge.

I'm going to leave you, she says to her lover: let me tell you a story about the time when we first met at the motel on L Street. A long time ago, before the Age of Man, when giants and dæmons lived in trees and tall hidden caves and the mountains pulled the days skyward and housed the gods, there was a girl with long brown hair and eyes like stars. "Eyes like stars?" Yes. She was the most beautiful girl of her tribe and she was kept locked inside a marble room, deep inside of the earth, inside of a basement or a mausoleum, with only the dead as her companions. And each night she cried out from her loneliness and from a quiet yet uninterrupted rage. "Why?" For the girl was unalive, of course, inside of the subterranean marble palace. She was rich. She was well fed: she ate red green and purple seeded grapes. She spit the grape seeds into hot bathing pools. She drank dark wines each night. She smoked the opium pipe. But she was alone, except for the unbodied dead, and the visits, each fortnight or sometimes only once in a month, when the dæmon would arrive in the costume of a husband and quietly put his cock into her sex. He rubbed her with his cock and sometimes, inside of the white rock underground palace, the earth would glide. But mostly, the girl rubbed her sex each afternoon and night, she touched her labia and clitoris and dreamed of a lover. And this rubbing of her labia and clitoris made a call through the stone and dirt and clay and a boy, the hunter, walking in the woods close to her prison one day, smelled the cunt, thought that he had discovered a treasure and stuck his sword into the ground where his body had led him and the gate to the prison opened and he saw the girl: naked on a white marble bed, her legs were splayed and her breasts fell to each side and her black-brown cunt moistly opened, he could see pink and knew, then, that his life had led him to this palace and he pulled his sword out of its sheath (for he had re-sheathed the sword when the gate swung wide) and he approached the girl and she smiled at him, opened her legs wider yet, pulled her labia apart, showed him the world and he, the hunter, her lover, showed then shoved his steel blade into the hole and the blood from her cunt and her breath while he did it, his breath and thrust, made nothing from nothing and everything amidst the wilds of their full-beating hearts.

The cunt now. The lips engorged and redder. She doesn't see her cunt, she doesn't take a mirror after fucking her lover on the workroom floor and peer between her legs, feet flat, knees wide to see the wideness the lover made in her today. She asks him what does it look like? And he—Redder. —Are they all like that? He won't tell her, walks away from her, turns the music on, it plays loudly about a lucky man, returns to his work station and she lies naked on the workroom floor still, his semen drips from her cunt onto the blue sheet and she is angry with him and he is angry with her and neither can ascertain why it is that the lover makes the beloved into the possessed one, the dæmon has come into her, possesses her now, rides her like an animal and the dæmons will carry out their battle of wills of wants of suck my cocks of my cunt needs your mouth; mother; here, now *now*.

She pulls off her clothes and drops them onto the floor. I don't love you, she thinks. He is naked in bed already, how would you like to fuck? he asks of her. She knows what she would like, says —I don't know. She straddles him, his cock is half-hard, she pushes her ass toward his face, her cunt lips hang down and she imagines they slap against his face like water against the hull of a boat. She pushes her cunt onto him, she has presented herself to him. She can feel the hole of her cunt opening wide, a fourth eye, the eye itself; the body of knowledge; blood filled, blood gnosis. He uses his tongue and his fingers, a magician, to make the girl into a mare, to make the girl into a willow tree, to make her into wind and the crepuscule. She feels good. This is *good*, the thinks, when the language thoughts are moving inside of her. I love him, I love you, she says. We are in love.

He looks into her cunt, red, swollen, he has sucked her lips and clitoris for an hour. He makes her come three times and she is quiescent while he laps at her again, like a sweet dog. Ninety percent of the energy in the universe is unknown, whence does it come? whence does it travel? like the cunt, he says, infinitely expanding, both knowable, I suck your lips, I put my cock into the black red slit, and unknowable. Like the southern glaciers, he says, a yellow full-moon rise, wind, and what I feel without knowing it: love? The universe and your wet cunt is a fourth-eyed yes. And she is quiescent in his fat arms. She listens. Sleeps. Dreams of filled-up baskets and wind storms.

34

She looks at the unaroused cunt. The cunt is covered in black hair. The outer lips are pale-leg white and then change into darkbrown; the inner lips are black-edged and then brown and pink. The clitoris peeks out red of its darkbrown overcoat, pulls back at a rough touch like a tentative animal. She opens her sex with her fingers, licks smells her fingers, she loves the smell of her cunt, the cunt slit is pink-red, her own secretions aid in her movements; she licks her fingers, she uses the spit-covered fingers to finger the cunt. She has never looked closely at her cunt before, it is forbidden and she knows and as a girl she closed her legs; as a girl she was ashamed of her fat mound, her pubic hair, the smell when a boy would remove her pants, the fluids of the body. The lover has taught her to love her cunt because the cunt is her center, the cunt is pleasure, the cunt knows and knew him, picked him from a cavalcade of other men.

And before her lover there was the Punjabi lover and after the Punjabi there was a Lebanese.

The Punjabi was older than her by many years, his black hair had greyed in his ears and the hair covered the ears and jowls and he reminded her of her old grandfather. His penis was small and his paunch bigger than his sex. He laughed with her and he bought her red wine and he didn't hold her hand and never loved her or wanted to marry her or eat her cunt but,—but what? He charged her, he stormed the old and built-up barricade of doubt of obligation of misery of loneliness of dried up cunt of habit and marriage habits, of what, what in her mind, *was*. (She was lonely in bed on all of those nights masturbating while the husband and children slept in warm beds, the husband beside her, quiet; she was quietly desperate.) Is, he whispered, is in flux. And he flew through the night and day skies toward her city from his country and for one day he fucked her just the one time and fell asleep and she was left alone and she did not have an orgasm, her cunt was opened and slowly opened and closed like a disappointed child slowly opening and closing an empty box. But she waited for him, for weeks for months, she pined. She lost weight and suddenly she was slim and her eyes appeared larger in her head so that she was surprised to look at photographs of herself with the owl eyes the mouse eyes the black eyes widely opened as if in supplication, and hungry. He said, although he never spoke in this manner, you. And he called her, and she, silly inexperienced excited and mad, the girl became possessed by a dæmon, by desire: Yes, she responded, silently.

And the other? The Lebanese. His penis was small and his paunch was bigger also. She loved him; he was younger and he had suffered at the hands of his state and so she loved his suffering and his look at her, a look which she was never offered as an adolescent girl when her cunt hummed and her belly hanged fat over her skirts and trousers: *I desire you I would like to fuck you Your eyes are like stars beautiful girl brighter wild won't you why don't you arrive in me?* Your eyes, he said, are a train. All of those years in her secondary school and the cunt's song but no boys to play with, no look of this You, she was alone in her bed at night, in her bedroom with the dark green coverlet and the white narcissus and she would put her fingers onto her cunt lips, onto her clitoris, and think of her lover, a lover—invisible intangible, he was strong and he fucked her and she would do her homework and masturbate on the floor on top of her school papers.

The Lebanese put his small penis into her cunt and she rode on top of him like a girl on a large animal and his belly pushed into her cunt and belly and because he was small-cocked and because she had had her children and she was large-slitted, she couldn't feel his cock inside of her, not at all, or perhaps only the tiniest whisper of his sex friction like a wasp at her neck. His gaze made her come and she rode him, girl on the boy, and looked at him and the storms raged outside the windows of the hotel night and the thunder sounded and she was happy and came all over his tiny sex and belly, she was wetter than she had ever been, even wetter than with her lover now, who can say why? He made her cunt cells vibrate he made her hands shake with joy and she was out with him and wet and howling in her spirit, the thunder outside, she laughed and she frightened him with her laugh, her wet cunt, her insatiable and wet cunt: fuck me again, she said, please? And the sweet Arab boy, sweet violent selfish and cruel, a liar, lover with the long and invisible wounds browner scars said, listen, read to me from a book. I would like a story to while away the hours of this long and thunderous night.

And her foreign lover now, where are you from? Perhaps you are from inside of her, or you are the you she imagines, blue blind eyed, a little sad, strong armed, fat belly, you cut the woods, shape the pieces, sand, lift up your metal tools; you labor with you hands teeth and tongue. You are foreign to her and the city; you are in exile, first from love and later from joy.

35

The girl and her lover are in a sandwich shop in his city.
Today she has driven to see him, it is one of the many days
she has made the drive to put her body next to his body, her
arms on his belly-skin, his cock her throat. And they are waiting for their sandwiches to be prepared, he holds her hand
and they are talking, perhaps, about the approaching winter
storms. And she begins to feel the hum in her cunt while he
talks to her, the fluids descend and blood-filled now and she
is wet, she can tell, her jeans feel tighter than a moment ago
and then something else, like an electrical current perhaps,
moves in her body and moves out to him, the held-back held-
breath moment just before the trees move violently in the
wind, before the wind, the winter rains and he looks at her,
stops speaking, turns his head toward the sandwich maker
and smiles, moves his free hand to her sex and cups her sex
tightly. —We need to hurry, right darling? And the girl is
amazed, violently amazed, for this man, her lover, who has
felt these invisible lines in the before-rains water, felt her
pull and call to him and smiles into her blinking hiding eyes

now and she had never before believed it and she had never
before heard anyone say it to her—that she existed, that her
silent vibrations were real, were realer than reality, than the
surfaces, than her own mask and she looks down, smiles also,
knows something, knows that her lover can see her, that he
sees her with his wide mystical inside eyes.

36

Today she phoned the husband for she had dreamed of him last night and was feeling sad and sorry for herself that she would always be lonely, that no man would come and take care of her, that she had made a mistake in fucking her lovers while married to the husband. In her dream she was in her old home, the same home as always, the home which her parents sold after they divorced and she is walking down the wide tree-lined street that leads to her childhood street and the purple flowers are in bloom and the street is a purple canopy in her dream and the tarmac is flower colored and carpeted and now she can't remember, but she misses him, he is her archetypal father her son and brother: fuck me? she says, couldn't you, simply, fuck me again? He won't. He cannot. I want a divorce now, he says. I don't want to wait any longer (for he has waited six months since he first moved out). And she is crying into the phone, tells him that she dreamed of him and that is he sure? and he becomes angry with her—this whore who fucked all of the men while he paid the bills and cleaned the garden and fixed the house problems—You lost me, he says, a long time ago. I did? she is crying louder into the phone. Yes, he screams, yes and yes (and her demanding cunt, its lips seeking the men to suck and lick her happily). And she hangs up the phone, and strangely she is happier, albeit sad, for she must know who she is, and she must hear from him again and again and ask it of him again and again, not that he doesn't love her, not that she won't miss him, and perhaps for her lifetime—but that he has not (for many years), for he cannot, be a god for her, and she his god also: possessed, possessive, the energy moves between them amorally like dark energy, limitless, unorigined, is, this is always outside the routes of mob and majority.

She dreamed of her lover, she is dreaming every day and this is what she dreamed: I was traveling with you and even now, only moments after waking, my children stirring and saying that they are hungry! and I recall gazing at you within my dream and I looked into your eyes and inside your right eye there were three spheres instead of the usual one, three blue eyes inside the white of your eye, like small orbiting planets, and the other eye and all four seeing pupils and blue irises staring into me from their different angles, cockeyed. Then your wife sat down to eat with us with your daughters. And she was kind to me and she stroked her daughter's hair and I could see, in the dream, that she loved her child, and you had betrayed me in the dream, put your cock into two other girls' cunts and it was necessary, you said, and I awoke, disoriented and unsad, but angry also at you for cheating on me in my dream. And thinking of those spheres, each ball spinning in the outer space of your vision.

She gives up on people. She gave up on her husband. And now with the lover, she finds that she will give up on him, give him up if she must do it. And why must she do it? he is beautiful to her now, his fat hands, fatty belly, sorrowful and blue look. She hates him and she loves him, sweet bitter and she never loved her husband like this—comfortable?—and now with him she is angered she is the banshee she would like to fuck him now she would not like to fuck him now; fuck you, she thinks. And she is happy and she is unhappy; you see, she says to him, we are both thesis and antitheses; the opposite of the opposite. Now, she says. And then.

—You are demanding, he tells her. It is never enough. It? she says. And she recalls how her husband had also complained of this it and how this it was not enough, and this it follows behind each of her lovers. It. it. it. What do they mean? And of what are they afraid? I am tired. I have suckled my children. My sons are growing. Get inside, it is raining. She yells to them while they splash in mud and puddles in the garden.

None of the moral platitudes offer any comfort to her: I am a bad girl. I wronged you. I did the right thing. It is destiny. The husband is cruel and selfish. She is selfish and mean and breaks the old laws.

37

Today she wails she moans and she makes animal noises, the snot is on her face and tears and she is moaning and cries, cannot speak, for the river that is in her, her sadness, her grief, her fear, the wound the husband made today when he, almost as an aside, sent her the divorce papers through the mail and the girl then falls to pieces (falls out of love?), no, into pieces wholly, she moans she cries she is a small child again and cannot, whether or not she wishes to, follow the rules of the strong and civilized girl, cries while she purchases her groceries, cries at the check-stand, she is sobbing while she is paying and although she is horrified at herself, she has also been surprised by the kind and gentle look the bagger gave to her when he hands her her things.

She thinks with her cunt she thinks, while he is rubbing her clitoris with his tongue.
orgasm (breath)
electric
breathing with her cunt? cosmos

the man fucking her, the lover fucks her; heaving his whole body into her with his bodycock (perhaps women are more languaged than men? she thinks. She thinks of the little girls who chatter nonstop while the little boys play loudly. Her lover won't talk with her while they fuck, so she talks to herself about god about love about her lover about the husband about her daddy, but if she talks too much then she can't lift away and then she is more alone lonelier with his fingers his lips sucking playing her cunt and her thoughts like kites, the five and five hundred of them lifted above his face her body while he sucks her, hang over her, blown away then with the gust that the gods will turn upon her form, if she is lucky, if she can no longer speak think, moves outside of language and into being).

38

The space the lover makes in her is a wound; the husband also makes a wound and it pains her differently—however it is true that these two men wound her: the one because he leaves her, abandons her like a child is abandoned in the nighttime, and the other because he loves her perhaps she loves to be wounded, sees the blood, feels this pain, speaks with god and knows, then, that she lives, that she is dying also.

She is driving southward to see her lover. She is tired. The music plays loudly on her car radio as it usually does when she drives to see him. The sun sets behind her and the shadows of cars stretch in front of her like grey-blue giants speeding along the highway. The light is yellow-gold and the red sun sinks behind her shoulder blades. Two shadows run side by side her now, the simulacra of the cars, and her own car's shadow drives directly in front of her as if it leads her to the lover and she is tired. When she arrives to your workroom she is more tired yet and you open the door and smile and she is mean bitter hates that she has come here, hates that it is you who has made her unhappy, made her into a living woman, made her unmade her each day that you see and fuck her.

She is tired today. She has thrown a party for her youngest son, he is nine years old. Today she doesn't speak to the husband; yesterday she received the official marriage dissolution papers in the mail. Today they are legally divorcing and they are together in a wide and green park on a hillside, a view of the water in the distance, clouds in the sky, it is grey and cool beneath the trees where the party is held. The children arrive and they play on the long concrete slide and in the trees and run around crying loudly. She doesn't speak directly to the husband unless forced to do so for the sake of appearances; she speaks to the children to the parents and her nephew. She sings happy birthday to her son. She picks up wrapping paper and paper plates and plastic bottles half-filled with punch and water. She throws everything into the trashcans. She carries the opened presents and leftover cake to her car. She makes seven trips back and forth to her car and she puts everything inside of it. She doesn't speak to the husband. Yesterday the post arrived and among the bills and advertisements were included the marriage dissolution papers in a thick yellow envelope. The children leave with the husband after the party; she kisses them; she smiles; she shows them that she is happy that she is having fun with them. She drives southward to see you. She has been a good mother today. She did not cry in front of the other parents; she made her son happy on his birthday. She took pictures and lighted the candles. She drives and thinks that she is tired. You open the door to your workroom. You have found a babysitter for your daughters, you know that her husband is taking her into the courtroom, you have tried to comfort her on the phone and now in person. She doesn't smile when she sees you, she walks past you, pisses loudly in the toilet, doesn't look at you, hates you, says to you that she is tired, the drive, the party, your smell.

The lover takes her to a restaurant and tries to please her with expensive foods, but she is too tired or scared or bitter or lonely and soon, halfway through the meal, they are fighting bitterly, she cries into her food, does not eat her expensive foods and he is disgusted with her, tells her that nothing he does pleases her—enough, it is not enough, he says; that she is selfish and he pays the bill for the food and she gets up from the table and goes to the bathroom and pisses loudly and he waits for her outside of the bathroom and she is not looking at him, she looked at herself in the mirror in the public toilet at the crying girl, disheveled, her face is red and marked-up from the fatigue and tears and she does not look like the beautiful girl from the beginning of this book; she is old-looking, she looks defeated and her face has fallen down. She leaves the bathroom and he stands there waiting and she doesn't look at him and he turns, angry now, and walks away from her and she follows him and they walk for blocks late at night in the city, he walks three paces ahead of her, he doesn't hold her hand but makes sure that she is behind him and glances back at her making corners in her mind and they walk through the dark labyrinth which has become her life with the lover. There are bright streetlights and prostitutes and mendicants and she is behind him and thieves or theatre goers and they are walking this dark and cool October night. She begins to cry softly while he leads her down the dark path of her grief. She has never felt so aggrieved as she does now, the husband has sent her the legal papers to dissolve the marriage, the lover walks in front of her and she is his small dog and follows him obediently crying louder and louder into the dark night air, she is sobbing as she does through many pages of this book, cries out her old and newly made grief, her loss, her aloneness, the three steps of space between her and the lover make loneliness into three paces and she thinks that she won't be able to bear it, that she can't bear it, that he is killing her and she tells him finally, in the dark night, yells out his name and that why would he like to kill her, the shy reserved girl, the business woman, the tightly suited and serious girl, screams on the corner of the dark night that god damn him he is killing her and why? And perhaps she has frightened him, she herself is amazed at the girl she has become, an hysteric and she feels that she will fly apart, fall apart like she fell into love and she would like to die and she looks at the night sky, following him again on their journey through the city, that this pain is unbearable and makes a river in her body and her body is the river the pain and that there is nothing else except the night sky, the three paces like wounds between her and the lover, the black crows which fill all of the high trees and scream and cry throughout the night and in her dreams their caws continue for many days afterwards.

How can a book such as this one end? Will the girl and her lover marry and fight until they have died? Will the girl beg her husband to re-marry her and save her, finally, from the banshee which eats her stomach throat and spine? Will the girl find other lovers, more men, and then later tell a story about this time when pain and the wounds of the lover, the husband, the cunt itself is a wound, delimited all of the days? The girl looks up from where she stands, she is still in the scene with her lover on the streets of his city, it is night and she cries in the street and in vain and he stands three paces from her and he doesn't comfort her and she wonders how she has come to this moment, how their lovemaking on the floor of his workroom, those glorious eternal days, led them to this nighttime almost two years later, and how to make sense of it, make sense of her life and give it meaning; how to pull out of the labyrinth into the labyrinth, make the girl into the queen and the lover into her king and their children are by their side and he has not killed her on the morn and she has seduced him with her stories and the dervishes and the djinn and the sailors have all returned home to the beginning of the nights tonight.

She awoke on another today and her eldest son was crying in his sleep, she could hear him from her bedroom. She gets up from the bed, she is cold, it is a dark and grey day and she momentarily thinks it is the middle of the night still, but it is morning, it is almost seven o'clock and her boy cries and she is sad also.

He tells her of his dream, how he dreamt that he and his brother were walking in the hills alone and that his brother was hungry and how his brother told him in the dream that he would like to eat something and her son is sad, he says, that he has no food for him and that they are alone. She feels grief while he relates his dream, that her marriage came undone, that the words do not describe in her mind in this book what it is that has happened in her son's dream, in her soul? heart? the body. The guilt she feels that her boy suffers in the nighttime, that he and his brother walked alone.

She comforts him as she used to when he was very small and he allows it today, albeit a little shy or ashamed of his need for his mother and perhaps he won't allow it again, for he is getting older and more aware that his mother should not hold his form, cradle his legs, sit her belly her legs against his thighs his buttocks as they lie together in his still-warm night bed. She loves her boys, she thinks. Their forms alone, the body smells, lines and fat and muscle and stink and dirt and brown dirtied snotty noses and black thick fingernails and feet: their swearing, their large feet, their appetites and cries of pleasure and displeasure which she loves.

She thinks a yes. She watches a film late at night and in the film the two lovers are fucking. The woman sits on the man and she fucks him. She is insatiable and he tells her that she is insatiable and he smiles and it is this actor's smile and she remembers, suddenly, how it was why it is that she fucked her lovers during the ending years of her marriage. The actor's smile reminds her and she is happy a little bit watching the movie because she knows that she listened to a quiet need inside of her that loudly raged for years inside of her, she imagined the lovers and then lovers arrived from the river below her throat, down to the cunt it moved moves, in trees, called to the lover, to his workroom, to suffering and to this out-joy; to love. And she cannot say that it was worth it, the word "worth" makes her feel sad and makes her feel that she has failed, that she is a failure (her sons the husband what the neighbors will say will not say and school officials and her relatives). Worth and capital and business and business meetings and school meetings and doctors' appointments and dinners with married couples in fancy and expensive and clean and tight restaurants make her feel it again. She is a bad girl. She is no good. She is ugly alone horrible and her face has fallen down. She watches the film, it is an old Japanese film which caused a scandal many years ago for the manner in which it shows the lovers fucking loving without boundaries, the girl kills her lover in the film and eats his penis and she remembers what she knows, that a call came into her form, her cunt's smells and secretions calling to him to come and arriving to possess her to be possessed to suck her cunt every day every moment and they are eternal together, she is Leda's daughter and he arrives for her and steals her from Menelaus because a god has decreed it, because the lover has desired it, chose love over kingship and war-power (and then does the old city fall? does the lover unwittingly court his own demise—the beloved is always the destroyer, also). He doesn't tell her to stop it. He doesn't says that she wants too much (her father her husband the other lovers). He smiles. Her lover pulls her cunt to his mouth and eats her like a good boy. The actors are gods; the girl and her lover also.

39

Outside of the words between them breath arrives on the edges of the alphabet, around the o the u the i—such a white beautiful space between the ˙ and the ı of the third vowel: what mysteries lie there? what ecstasy? which god? There lie the girl and her lover, the mother and the son, the heroine and the hero in the dark invisible mirror eternal and

40

The girl is in a bar in her dream. She has awakened and that is all that she remembers of the place of the dream. She is in a bar and is the lover with her? She is alone and there are barwomen serving her drinks. Then she is standing behind the wide black bar-counter and looks down to see one of the barwomen looking up at her. The barwoman is squatting on the floor and the girl looks down into the large blue eye of a cyclops, the open blue orb blinks back at her from the middle of the pretty barwoman's forehead.

Then the girl awakens and rises from her bed, she is alone at home and will make coffee and puts the kettle on to boil water and walks to the back door of her home to let the dog outside and places her hand on the doorknob and feels a small pinch in her index finger and pulls her hand back quickly to pull what she imagines to be a thorn in the side of her finger out, and sees a black-yellow wasp stuck into the finger's flesh and she is frightened and blows the animal away from her body, shakes the hand and the finger begins to throb and she wonders about the cyclops about the wasp on the underside of the doorknob and she has no idea what these things may or may not mean, if they are symbols, the one pulled from the unconscious and the other from her life as she moves through her days.

41

Because on that evening ooo pages ago when the girl and her
lover were walking in the late-night black labyrinth of her
grief and sorrow and rage, as she walked three paces behind
her lover, silently, in the dark grey night, the girl called out in
her mind to the dead and foreign grandmother, screamed in
the inside universe to her that she cannot bear it, Nene, that
she will not be able to live; that, on some day (not today), —
Please don't take my mama from me. Please, Nene —she
begged her, —promise me in your dead and ghost language
that you won't do it, that you must know that I cannot bear
it, to live in the world without Maman on some future allot-
ted day. At the labyrinth's center, the minotaur leads her to the
mother's corpse and mounts the dead mother and says *some
day* and the girl screams at him and kills him with her hands,
sucks his cock dry, cuts it off, she is a maenad, she kills the
beast, she is intoxicated, mad, not for the mother, she must
have her mother, this is the loss she cannot bear, she will not,

Nene, blooded and tired, screams and howls into the night,
three paces from her lover, he looks back at her, marks her
passes, and she mourns the undead mother whose death,
tonight, she will not ever be able to abide.

42

She arrives at his workroom. It has been one week since she last saw him, when he crossed the Styx to find her, begged the underworld gods to release his beloved and then led her through the valley, along the dark night streets, pulled her hand and they walked together up the steep paths where she then lay, howling, and he, as in the myth, kills her that night in October, looked upon her and she was stone and he left there alone on the dark streets and she fell back down into the underworld.

Today they are together again. And she smiles at him, he takes her hand and kisses her aggrieved fingers. He lies on the bed naked and she straddles him. She puts her back to him, bends down and her ass and her long black cunt lips kiss his face. She is sucking his small cock and then she is lying on his thighs and biting marks into them and he is tonguing her cunt and she imagines or she knows that her cunt is the mouth and she and he are kissing like sweet bodied lovers on his bed, they embrace like this: his tongue and her clitoris and labia and she opens her mouth at his thighs widely and she is howling into the night or grunting or smiling or she sings into his cock-light: he makes her again into his beloved, he makes her into happiness and a red portal, he knows her and she needs him and she knows, then, inside of pleasure, fuck me again she says and he cannot for five minutes and then she sucks him and she climbs on top of him, like the girl in the Japaneses film and she faces him now and rides him and her cunt is full, not only with cock, but with all of the blood in the veins and just the cock inside of her and she is coming and opens her grinning mouth, closes her red and hungry cunt around his cock and feels then, afterwards, contented, drowsy, she falls asleep immediately and like on a hot lazy summer afternoon, wishes for no other thing or man or life.

43

She takes her boys to visit her father and aunt and uncle for a scene in this book. Her sons are wild and loud and dirty and do not listen when she scolds them and they break the aunt's crystal glasses or watch television for hours or interrupt constantly during the evening conversations and hit each other and laugh loudly and complain that they are too bored. And she is embarrassed and ashamed and she remembers now, her aunt and uncle begin talking about her childhood and her parents' divorce and the sad years when the girl's mother and father did not speak to one another, fought over her and her sister, over the house, over the cutlery and cups and plates and all division of goods, and she refeels the grief of it, the howl of it which still howls inside of her and she knows that she is still that girl when she visits her aunt and uncle, that her forty years fall down the well into the ten-year-old girl, the girl who was quiet, who was ashamed, who did not speak and who watched her parents pull each other out and into pieces of themselves, poor and drunken and saddened and distant (the father then moved to another state) and enraged and faulted and a failure and liars and lonely and bitter and sad (again), and then the mother without money and bill-collectors and the screaming the whores the bitches at the father who pushed the mother against the walls and the walls the windows later barred and fallen and decrepit, as she is now looking into her old aunt's face and the more-wrinkled face now with the years which pass but the father is the same and the mother also in her mind or imagination or soul or selfness—all of the fathers are her father, and all of the lovers are her lover, and her lover and father fuck her in her sleep, look into her face, aging, kinder, and the new father whom she visits now with her boys at her aunt and uncle's house in Los Angeles is unfamiliar to her, his wrinkled face and sadder brow and kinder and quieter and balder form, and she can't say who he is but only that he reminds her, vaguely, like a blurred charcoal drawing, of the man who is her Father, who regards her still inside of her unguarded places while she sleeps.

She dreams then of her mother and in her dream the mother is singing. The mother is young, as she remembers her from her childhood days, girlhood days, the black hair and straight cut fringe and thinner body, large fat breasts and in her dream she sees her mother's naked ass and long legs and the mother holds a microphone to her mouth, sucks upon it and sings and her voice is the most beautiful voice that she can imagine, more beautiful, even, of course, than it was then when she was a girl and her mother was younger and she sings and

125

the crowd applauds wildly, and the mother is herself, she has not aged, she is not decrepit, she does not approach her seventy-second year and the pains in her hips and knees. She is not fat. She does not stink of old age. She is not tired, irritable and lonely. She does not live in another American country. She is fresh. Kind. Beautiful like a fresh black flower. Eternal mother; ancient singer.

44

The terror of childbirth returns to the girl today and she cannot say wherefore. When her second boy was born she suffered; there was pain. And just before the boy emerged, before he passed through the portal of her vagina and before she knew that he was a boy (he was a girl in her mind all of the months of her pregnancy, she gave him a girl's name and future) but after he had pushed himself from her cervix, and she is out of control, the body the boy, and her husband was sitting behind her, younger, delighted, anticipated his breath, held to see his second child, and the midwife in front of her, and she saw for eternity's second or minutes in the room's high corner, a vision of the blood stretched out toward infinity, her bloodlines in a line of people and they opening the blood for the boy to come through her and the vagina becomes the monstrous sacred mouth on that Tuesday in October.

The night after the boy was born she dreamed of a devil. Her baby was the devil in her dream and screamed and mucus

poured from his mouth and nose and his head twisted un-
naturally left and right until it swung around like a girl on a
swing. She was afraid in her dream and afraid, also, that she
hated her child, the child she had just birthed, the boy she
did not want (she wanted to sleep, to be free) and the opened
cunt the wide vaginal walls and bloody and torn labia wel-
comed to the world the boy, the birth is the opening, the dead
in a queue in a high corner of the living room and the terror
that the birth incites, the gods standing and see the girl in
pain, the cervix pulls open to let the babe out and the obliv-
ion then during her labor, she spins off, she heaves, the body
heaves, the muscles contract and the body knows, not the
girl, how the child must be birthed, how the girl must sur-
render to the body to the gods to the strict and straight pole-
light which slammed down her head via the throat heart
lungs stomach uterus to the cunt to open the ancient path
and the flesh emerged from flesh and the girl was terrified,
understood why it was that doctors gave the mothers drugs
to not know not feel that the mother is the god, that the gods
await, stand in line, blackness, light, and the dead, the new
breathing blue boy who screamed out when he emerged.

She was relieved after she pushed him out. Light and free, until he cried, until she dreamed the devil's dream.

She remembers her childhood, and the mother's black fringe
like a belt across her face. She remembers the father's hands
in punishment; she remembers the rules of their house. She

remembers that after the father left their house the rules also left and then she and the mother and sister moved from the house and into an apartment and later into another apartment. She remembers television and all of the shows and how each day after school she would turn on the animated box and watch the shows until eleven o'clock at night and how if anyone asked her if she were happy she would answer in the affirmative and how, now, when she returns to the aunt's house she asks them to turn it on, that she would like to sit in front of it, that she is very happy with her life and her family and that she loves them all and can we, please, watch more TV? (and leave this city and decrepit remembering family, her running screaming boys, behind).

So that she hates the lover she loves him. She would like him to suffer she suffers when he is suffering. She wants to hurt him with her words and then whip him and why is this love and she thinks her anger her sorrow her passion for a man who does not arrive for her when he arrives for her she would not like to love him.

45

The girl is fighting again with the lover. She is enraged, she is the banshee, wails upon him, sends him her wails like she does her piss, she pisses on him today after their row, he tells her to do it, he drinks her urine, sucks it, gurgles it, closes his eyes and eats from her body, her kidneys, her cunt.

First there is a fight at a pub. It is not the pub which they met in at the front of this book, but a pub in his city. It is an English-style place, and there are many beers to choose from and he eats a hamburger while she wails at him, she is not hungry, how can you eat? she asks of you. She cries into her pint of beer, she orders another beer, cries to him. —Why don't you love me enough? Why have you abandoned me again? Why don't you leave your wife, the bitch, for me? For me? And she tells him how she will find other lovers, how there are men she would like to fuck and fuck you if you don't love me enough and he looks at her, she screams at him quietly, the good quiet girl-child, and his blue-white irises, the planets swirling inside of the orbits of his eyes, the wide blue white blue gaze; he looks at her quietly, quiescently, —If I leave her to marry you, you'd better not ever leave me.

And then they remove their clothes an hour later and I'm cold, she tells him, and too bad, take them off and he pulls her into the bathroom of his workroom and he lies on the floor of the toilet and orders her and do it, he says, piss onto me. She squats over him, caresses his lips with her cunt lips and begins to pass her urine into his mouth, she will decide when he breathes, when he can live, and his mouth is urine-filled and she can see white bubbles surfacing in his mouth at the surface of her yellow piss and he is drinking her urine, to live, and she continues the pissing. And then, after he fucks her in the shower, he will beat her with the black whip and she will cry to him and then he will put his cock into her again and she will hold him and then he will put his mouth to her cunt and his fingers inside of the cunt and arousing her clitoris and the coin-size balloon inside of her and she will shake from it, the legs spasm and move up and down rhythmically and later she falls asleep with him. Amazed and violently alive.

131

46

Now the girl returns from another long journey, it is the last journey in this book. She is riding in an airplane high above her country. She cannot feel her cunt's desires now. She has not seen her lover in many weeks and until he puts his penis inside of her cunt she doesn't know how or who she is. She is not herself until then now. Until he makes her again into the new girl she is.

She saw an old friend in another American city. And her friend looked haggard and lonely tired. Her classmate from middle school sat before her, face fallen down, the eyes sunken and black bags beneath them and her hair mostly greyed. We are getting old, she thought; my friend looks old. What happened to the girlfriend she was? The girlfriend who laughed out loud too much and who, brushing her hair back from her face again and again in middle school, made faces at the world, was angered at the injustices of history of men of her own lying cheating father and who was going *to do* things, —this old haggard woman didn't laugh today as they sat together in the café. Her girlfriend talked for hours about her husband and the unhappy marriage and the sweet performing high-achieving children and the broken-down house they were fixing and the troubles with jobs, the mean bosses she encountered, the TV shows that she and her children enjoyed.

What is it? thinks the girl, in her girlfriend's face that so terrifies me? Something her friend said about *the paths not taken*, some small and over-used meaningless phrase, or the slow sad fat fat-filled TV watching beaten down middle class life—of vacuous conversations or TV lives of suburban tight-coat requirements for living, the morality as grim and severe as the weather in the girlfriend's cold eastern city, albeit invisible, albeit the paths were taken widely eyes opened to them.

My cunt has died? I need my lover now in his absence, inside of his absence I love him passionately, to kill adore him, to spend my life in between his legs and not to end all of this— all of our passionate desires—in a heap of disappointed and disillusioned half phrases; this what the girl thinks on her airplane ride across her country, the rivers and mountains below her feet, beneath the metal and air and cloud.

133

(Her friend doesn't fuck her husband.) —I am not so sexual, she says. I don't desire him. (Or: *we forget to have sex*.)

While the girl is in the distant city, she meets a friend of her lover's for a drink at a pub and he tells her stories about her lover. He asks her questions also, seeking, it seems, the lover, the girl, inside of the stories inside of his own mind. And then the friend of her lover's tells her about another girl in Paris whom her lover dined with while traveling there for work for woods and how when the lover met the French girl in the office building told the French girl that her breasts were lovely like small Parisian stars. And the girl is enraged now in the pub, would like to kill her lover, thinks that she is also ashamed, thinks that he doesn't love her, thinks that he will lie to her and cheat her, like she has lied and lies and cheated cheats the husband and she stays late in the bar talking and flirting with the barman after the friend of her lover departs.

47

She dreams of her lover. And in her dream he is fucking her and they are together and she is happy. And then she awakens and the usual black melancholy of missing him of not having him of her talismanic loneliness begins, descends as she ascends from the dreamworld and becomes slowly aware of the outside world of her arm and her head which lie to-day on the lover's chest,—that his arm is around her, that he is warm holds her and they are naked beneath his woolen blankets on the floor of his workroom; it is six o'clock in the morning and they are together and in love and have spent the night together and he fucked her in the middle of the night, stuck it into her while she slept and she is happiest than she can ever remember and for the first time in her memory her inner cosmos the dream-lover and her outside life, her white skinned blue-eyed fat bellied lover meet have merged at the top of her skin inside of her sex which is inside outside of her body her mind or the spirit and she has taken communion with him, lost her mind and given her flesh for his, for this, today.

48

Is it true that she loves him like this, or is it the illusion of the story which renders the girl, the lover, the husband and children to entertain the listener, the reader, the eavesdropper. Or is he her grand love, she loves him with the passion of the gods; she opens her legs for him; runs from him; becomes the willow the mare the stone creature for him each day each breath each written etched stone word on tombstones on ancient carved stone crosses on the indecipherable stelae on the backs of her stony thighs. She is filled with him with god.

This is the stepping out, *ekstasis*—these words these white spaces on the page that make the book make the world, make the gods descend into cock and cunt. I am a woman I am a man a child an old lady dog: see me, the girl says, I am happy. I am filled up with cock; I put my cock into the lover on these pages; and the lover, you, you put your cock into me. We are free. Blind. Stupid and god loves us and god has made us into his acolyte, put the girl and the lover onto his path, inside of his breath, ministering to the living the dead, the trees and the black crows in a northern city who come down twice a year to caw and scream throughout the late afternoons beneath the impending crepuscule.

And what of the story about the blond? (or the black?), tell about them also, the girl demands; or the man I met only briefly in a business meeting and how we fell in love and how we didn't fuck one another or kiss and I held his hand only one time, late at night, on the darkest streets of the city and so he took my hand and carried me along in his handsome embrace. Or. And I fell in, with the blond, the black, the Punjabi, a Lebanese, the lover—And. With you also, with the writer who writes, the hand which sings, the maker of phrases who makes me, the girl in this book, beautiful brown-eyed girl from the beginning of a romance, standing in front of a mottled and grey mirror with her lover before he is the lover. Her face has not fallen down and the girl has not fallen into love, not yet, in a few moments more, 135 pages ago, the lover will remove her clothes and she will lie back on the motel bed on L Street and spread her legs and breathe live for this interlude, which could be eternity, which could be an ecstatic's confession, later, now, today as the writer makes them, girl and her lover, mother and son, queen to the ancient sun king, to the satyr the god the dæmon, while he rubs sucks and licks her cunt.

SELECTED DALKEY ARCHIVE PAPERBACKS

SELECTED DALKEY ARCHIVE PAPERBACKS

SELECTED DALKEY ARCHIVE PAPERBACKS

FOR A FULL LIST OF PUBLICATIONS, VISIT: WWW.DALKEYARCHIVE.COM